D0383884

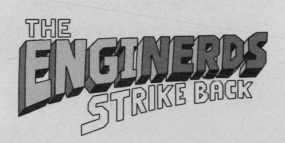

Also by Jarrett Lerner

EngiNerds
Revenge of the EngiNerds
Geeger the Robot Goes to School
Geeger the Robot: *Lost and Found*
Give This Book a Title!

Coming soon

The Hunger Heroes: *Missed Meal Mayhem*

THE ENGINERDS STRIKE BACK

JARRETT LERNER

Aladdin

NEW YORK   LONDON   TORONTO   SYDNEY   NEW DELHI

ALADDIN

An imprint of Simon & Schuster Children's Publishing Division
1230 Avenue of the Americas, New York, New York 10020
First Aladdin paperback edition February 2022
Text copyright © 2021 by Jarrett Lerner
Illustrations copyright © 2021 by Serge Seidlitz
Also available in an Aladdin hardcover edition.

For information about special discounts for bulk purchases,
please contact Simon & Schuster Special Sales at 1-866-506-1949
or business@simonandschuster.com.
The Simon & Schuster Speakers Bureau can bring authors to your live event.
For more information or to book an event contact the Simon & Schuster Speakers
Bureau at 1-866-248-3049 or visit our website at www.simonspeakers.com.
Cover designed by Karin Paprocki
Interior designed by Hilary Zarycky
The text of this book was set in Amasis.
Manufactured in the United States of America 0122 OFF
2 4 6 8 10 9 7 5 3 1
The Library of Congress has cataloged the hardcover edition as follows:
Library of Congress Control Number 2021931772
ISBN 978-1-5344-6934-1 (hc)
ISBN 978-1-5344-6935-8 (pbk)
ISBN 978-1-5344-6936-5 (ebook)

For River

Preface

I'VE GOT GINGER ALE UP MY NOSE, applesauce in my eye, and a smear of ketchup across my forehead.

My best friend, Dan, looks like he got his head dunked in a vat of strawberry jam.

And the rest of our friends?

Well, they don't look much better.

Jerry's covered in juice.

John Henry Knox is smothered in mustard.

And if you wrung out Edsley's hair, you'd have enough chocolate syrup to make every one of us a milkshake.

Out of all of us, Mikaela fared the best—but even she could use a fresh pair of clothes.

It feels strange to be thinking of her, Mikaela, as a friend. Twenty minutes ago, I thought of her as more of an enemy.

But that's not even close to the strangest part of the moment, as we all stand there together on Feldman's

Field, surrounded by the metal pieces of a broken-down robot, the dozens of pounds of meat he'd been stuffing himself with for the past several days, and an assortment of now-empty bottles and cans and boxes and jars of beverages and condiments that we just battled him with.

No, the strangest part by far is the spaceship that just touched down on the field's patchy grass, and the alien who emerged from it in order to inform us that our planet is in grave danger and will be reduced to dust within a week.

Oh, wait.

My bad.

He said TWO weeks.

If we're lucky . . .

Confused?

Well, yeah—so am I.

There are a couple books you can read to clear up any confusion you have about the bot. All I'll say here is that he was one of eighteen such machines designed, built, and programmed by Dan to eat and compress and store food for humans, and that, after malfunctioning in a rather spectacular fashion (that is, *farting* that compressed food out at humans), we had to battle sixteen of them in the alleyway behind our town's grocery store, the Shop & Save. That should've been the end of that. But then Mike Edsley—the stupidest smart kid in the galaxy—built and loosed his robot, Number 17, on our town. It took several days to find and deal with that bot, named Klaus—who's now, thankfully, lying in pieces at our feet.

And Robot Number 18?

That bot was never built. Dan, Jerry, John Henry Knox, and I split its parts up into four piles and each took one. I packed my pile into a box, cinched it shut with about thirty yards of duct tape, and shoved it under my bed—*way* under my bed—where the collection of metal can never cause trouble again.

But back to more pressing matters.

Like the alien.

And our apparently doomed planet.

Though I'm afraid I can't clear up any of your confusion about all of that. Because about those matters, I'm as in the dark as anyone. And speaking of the dark—even though I kind of just want to run home, crawl into the cozy dimness beneath my bed, cuddle up with that box of robot parts, and hide for the next couple weeks . . . even though, after having only just finished solving one huge problem (Klaus), I don't think I have it in me to deal with another, even *huger* problem. . . . I also don't really want to be reduced to dust along with the entire planet.

So I take a deep breath.

Rub the applesauce out of my eye.

And take a step closer to the alien . . .

1.

THE ALIEN, I SHOULD SAY, DOESN'T LOOK LIKE

an alien.

Like a *movie* alien, I mean.

The kind you see in old TV shows and on the covers of certain science fiction books.

If you walked past this alien on the street, you probably wouldn't bat an eye. I bet you could even have a quick conversation with him—about the weather, maybe, about the big, somewhat strange-looking cloud you've seen floating around in the sky lately—and you wouldn't think twice of it.

Sure, his eyes are a bit big.

His nose is a tad narrow.

His skin has an odd green-blue tinge to it.

And his voice carries a slight squeak.

But otherwise, he looks and sounds and moves just like a normal kid.

And *farts* like one too.

A fact that I managed to entirely forget, even though

only moments ago he let a particularly foul one loose with a long, loud *FFFfffpffweeeeeeeeeeeeeeeeeeeeeeee*-PARP!

I guess learning that your planet is a week or two away from being utterly destroyed can do some damage to your short-term memory.

But that bold step I just took toward the alien landed me right in the fetid heart of his otherworldly fart cloud.

I leap back, gagging, before the gas can utterly destroy my lungs.

"Sorry," the alien says. "Those Food-Plus veggie burgers are *really* not sitting well."

"So that *was* you."

It's Mikaela. And though I've got my eyes squeezed shut, worried as I am that the intergalactic nastiness that recently leaked out of the alien's backside might melt my corneas, I can tell that Mikaela's brain is spinning fast as it finally, at long last, puts together the pieces of this puzzle that we've all been driving ourselves crazy over for the past few days.

"You took all that food from the Food-Plus," she says. "And—"

"Yes," the alien interrupts.

And I crack open my eyes just in time to see him say:

"I caused the blackout. And I made that satellite fall out of the sky, too."

He's talking about the out-of-the-blue blackout that left our town without power for two whole hours, and the satellite—you know, those big contraptions that spin around in *outer space*—that came plummeting out of the sky and crashing in, again, *our* town. A pair of crazy, inexplicable events that I'd been so sure were caused by Edsley's rogue robot.

"But those were both accidents," the alien continues. "The other stuff wasn't."

John Henry Knox steps forward, now that the creature's fart has cleared.

"*What* other stuff?" he asks.

"The precipitation," the alien says. "All that snow. And the rain behind that other food store the other day."

He means the "freak blizzard" that caused our town to cancel school yesterday—in *the middle of May*—and the sudden, super-intense downpour that drenched me, Dan, Jerry, John Henry Knox, and the last of the butt-blasting bots in back of the Shop & Save.

"You . . . ," I say, remembering that day, recalling the fear I felt thinking that my life as I knew it was about to come to a screeching halt as those bottomlessly hungry, dangerously flatulent robots overtook us and then took over our town, our country, and maybe even the whole entire world. "You *saved* us," I finally finish.

The alien nods.

Then says:

"And I came down here to try to help do it again."

2.

"BUT..."

The alien pauses and peers around at the neglected expanse of Feldman's Field.

"This may not be the best place to explain the situation," he says.

I think I get what he means. While the field, overgrown and out of the way as it is, isn't exactly one of our town's most popular destinations, if anything's going to get people flocking to it, it's an enormous cloud-draped spaceship.

"My ship can't stay on the ground for too long," the alien adds. "It's against protocol. And I really can't be caught breaking protocol."

I wonder if his ship has some sort of autopilot feature, so the alien can send it back up into the sky and stay here on the ground with us. Or maybe it's got a cloaking device, a button he can press that'll make the ship completely invisible.

The alien doesn't tell us. Instead he takes a step

directly toward Dan.

"Dan . . . ," he says, swinging an arm out toward his ship. "Would you care to join me?"

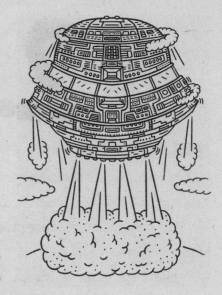

As soon as I understand what the alien is suggesting—that Dan board the ship with him and head up into the sky—sirens start going off in my brain, bright red lights flash, and I think, *No. No, no, no, no, no, no, NO.*

I turn to Dan.

His eyes are as wide as waffles.

"Um," he says. "Ahhh . . ."

"I'll explain everything," the alien says. "And you can report back to your friends as soon as we're through. Though it may take several hours. There's a lot to explain. But the future of your planet depends upon it."

"Bahhh . . . ," Dan responds.

My tired brain—remember, we just finished hunting down and battling a super hangry robot—kicks into overdrive, trying to find a different option, one that doesn't involve my best friend traveling tens of thousands of feet up into the air with an alien we only just met.

But before I can think of a thing, Dan steps forward and says, "Yeah. Okay. I'll do it."

"Dan—" I say. "You don't—"

"It's cool, Ken," he interrupts. Then he tips his head toward the alien. "He's already helped us so much. We can trust him."

I take a deep breath—and a rush of pins-and-needles nervousness fills my body up along with the air. I consider arguing with Dan. But I know him. Better than anyone. I know that look in his eyes. He's made up his mind. And once Dan has made up his mind about something? Look out. If single-handedly building a fleet of walking, talking—and, yes, farting—robots doesn't prove as much, then I don't know what does.

"Come over as soon as you're done," I tell him.

"Of course," Dan says.

Giving my shoulder a squeeze, he turns toward the alien. He nods, gulps . . . and strides toward the spaceship. We all watch him climb the ramp that leads up to the ship's doorway, keeping just a couple steps behind the alien. He stops at the very top of the ramp and turns to give us a quick wave.

I think Dan must be the bravest kid—no, the bravest *person*—in the world. Brave enough to board an alien's spaceship and briefly—at least, I hope it's brief—*leave* this world.

I think this—and then watch Dan step through the doorway and disappear into the ship. A beat later, the door closes and is then quickly covered up by a swirl of cloud. And it's only a couple seconds after *that* that the ship, as noiselessly as the beating of a butterfly's wings, lifts off the ground and sails up into the sky.

3.

I STARE, SQUINTING, UP AT THE CLOUD-
covered spaceship as it rises, rises, and rises some more.
It takes less than a minute for it to reach the lowest of
the *real* clouds in the sky. And then it's gone, blended
seamlessly with the rest of the white and gray puffs
looming above us.

I'm about to lift my fingers to my mouth so I can
gnaw on my nails—a nervous habit that I actually
thought I'd kicked years ago—when Mikaela's voice
stops me.

"Well . . ."

She lowers her own gaze from the sky.

It takes a minute for me to do the same, and another
for all the other EngiNerds to do so too. No doubt
everyone's mind is turning over the same series of
questions mine is.

Is Dan going to be okay?

Can we really trust this alien?

Why is he here?

What the heck is threatening our planet?

Mikaela plants her hands on her hips and scans the field around her.

"I guess," she says, "we should clean this place up."

No one moves.

And it doesn't take a genius to know what everyone's thinking *now*.

Why bother cleaning up Feldman's Field if the junky stretch of patchy grass might just be reduced to dust in a week or two?

"Suit yourselves," Mikaela says. "But *I'm* not about to start acting like a jerk."

She scoops up an empty juice box off the ground and chucks it toward the nearest trash can. It hits the rim with a *THUNK* and bounces in.

Edsley joins her a second later, grabbing the bottle of chocolate syrup he battled Klaus with.

It takes only a few more seconds before all the rest of us join in. We clean up our mess and then some, leaving that old, overgrown field that no one even goes to anymore looking even better than we found it.

4.

ONCE WE'VE CLEANED UP THE WATER BOTTLES

and juice boxes and soda cans and milk cartons, once we've tossed out the meatball subs and double-stacked burgers and strips of bacon and links of sausages that the endlessly hungry Klaus has been feasting on and compressing in his stomach for the past few days, the only thing that's left to deal with is the robot himself.

One by one, we gather around him.

The *pieces* of him, that is.

Because thanks to some quick tool work by Max, Amir, Alan, and Simon, plus some expert directing by Mikaela, the robot is now broken down into a harmless heap of parts. A head. A torso. A pair of arms. A couple of legs. And two feet. So long, Mr. Where's the Beef.

"What," asks Jerry, "are we supposed to do with *him*?"

It's a good question.

An *important* question.

And so even though my thoughts keep getting

tugged up toward
the clouds and how
Dan's faring among
them, I try to prop-
erly consider the
question.

My first idea is to bring the broken-down bot to a foundry and have him liquified into an even more harmless puddle of molecules.

Unfortunately, I've got no clue where the nearest foundry is. And even if there just so happens to be one around the corner, I doubt whoever is running the place would let a bunch of kids waltz in and access their two-thousand-something-degree fire.

My next best idea is to split the bot up, just like we did with the one that was never built. Jerry can take the arms and legs. Mikaela can have the torso. John Henry Knox can have the head. And I guess I'll take the feet. Maybe I'll give them to my dog, Kitty. The pooch's all-time favorite toy is a dirty sock that he found under a super disgusting Dumpster. His favorite pastime is licking our kitchen's a-little-less-disgusting-than-a-Dumpster-but-not-exactly-immaculate linoleum floor. I'm sure he'd find *something* to love about a pair of robot feet.

I'm about to share this plan with everyone else, but Edsley jumps in before I can get a word out.

"I'll take him."

I look over at Edsley and find him staring down at the broken-down bot with a glint in his eye.

It makes me nervous.

Really nervous.

He must feel my eyes on him, because he looks up and says, "He *is* mine."

If I hadn't just helped battle the bot, if I hadn't just seen a spaceship sink down from out of the sky and land a few dozen feet away from me, if I hadn't just *met an alien* and found out that our planet was in danger of being reduced to dust in a week or two, if my body didn't feel like a bunch of stapled-together noodles and my brain didn't feel like a scoop of cold mashed potatoes, if I weren't severely scared and distracted due to the fact that my best friend is currently floating around somewhere in the sky with an alien we only just met, I might put up more of a fight.

But instead I choose to go with the simplest plan, the easiest option, the one that doesn't involve *me* doing any work or taking on any responsibility. I tell Mike, "Fine. Whatever."

"Noice," Edsley says, grinning down at the bot.

A wave of panic whips through my body.

And before Edsley can gather up *all* the pieces of the bot, I nudge him aside and grab a few for myself. One arm. One leg. A random assortment of screws, nuts, and bolts.

"Dude," says Edsley. "You *just* said I could have it."

"You can," I say, lifting up the bot's arm. "This is just a little insurance."

"Insurance?"

"Against your idiocy."

Now it's Edsley's turn to say, "Whatever." He mutters it moodily as he gathers up the last pieces of Klaus.

5.

AS SOON AS HE'S GOT THE REST OF KLAUS
bundled up in his arms, Edsley heads off in the direction
of his house, not even bothering to say bye to any of us.

"Mike!" I call after him. "THINK before you ACT!
DON'T do anything STUPID! PLEASE!"

He flicks a hand up into the air to acknowledge that
he heard me.

Or maybe it's more of a leave-me-alone gesture.

I heave a sigh and turn back to the others.

I find Mikaela staring up at the sky again. Maybe
trying to see if she can spot the cloud that isn't a cloud
at all but is, in fact, a spaceship. Maybe hoping that the
cloud is already on its way back down to us, to return
our friend and clue us in as to just what is going on.

But the alien said that it might take several hours to
explain the situation to Dan, and it's only been, like,
twenty-five minutes.

All of which makes me want to gnaw my fingernails
down to nubs again.

Mikaela lowers her eyes and looks at me.

"This is gonna be the longest wait in history," she says with the tiniest hint of a smile. A smile that I can tell is forced.

"Tell me about it," I say. I try to push my lips into a little smile too but totally fail.

Mikaela checks the sky again.

"But I guess that's all we can do," I say. "Wait."

"Wait," Mikaela says, "and rest."

She turns to me again. This time, though, her smirk is gone. There isn't the slightest trace of it.

"We're gonna need it," she says seriously. "I don't know what this threat to the planet is. But as soon as we find out, we're going to have to work our butts off to do away with it."

She's right, of course. Though as long as Dan is still up there in the sky, I doubt I'll be getting any rest.

6.

WE ALL SPLIT UP AND HEAD HOME.

I take it slow.

Reee-e-e-ee-eee-eeeeally slow.

I've got so much stuff banging around in my head, and I'm pretty sure the longer I'm cooped up in my house, the crazier I'll go and the more terrified I'll be.

Because *something* out there is apparently threatening the continued existence of our planet.

And we, the EngiNerds, are supposed to help put a stop to it?

That right there is more than enough to cause some terror.

I mean, we're *kids*.

Yeah, sure—smarter-than-average, mechanically and technically proficient kids.

But still *kids*.

And due to that, I highly doubt, whatever the threat is, we're going to have much luck convincing any adults to help us out. What are we supposed to do, tell our parents or the police that there's this big cloud that's actually a spaceship, and that the alien piloting the thing around came down to Feldman's Field to tell us that our planet is in serious danger? Mm-hmm. Like *that's* going to work.

But there's no point dwelling on all that just yet, not when we don't even know the specifics of the problem we're dealing with. So I do my best to shove the crazy-making thoughts and panic-inducing terror away. I remind myself that, in addition to being the bravest person in the world, Dan might also be the most *brilliant*. If he says we can trust this alien, we can.

So I get back to my snail-paced walk home.

I linger.

I loiter.

I dilly-dally.

I dawdle.

And I guess I do a good job of it.

Because soon enough, I don't even have to *try* to delay.

Suddenly, I can't help but do it.

It's a tree that does it to me first.

Not a particularly special tree.

Just . . .

. . . a tree.

You know, a trunk and a bunch of leaves and some branches.

But looking at the tree, and at the same time thinking about the fact that *something* is threatening to obliterate it—that makes the tree seem like nothing short of a miracle.

And then everything else is seeming miraculous too.

Not just all the other trees.

But the bushes.

And the flowers.

And the birds.

And every single individual blade of grass.

Even the cars passing by and the stores across the street.

And all the people, too, everyone so busy living their lives, looking at their phones or zipping by on their bikes or sipping coffee or nodding their heads along to whatever's playing in their earbuds or cars.

We're all here, together, in this moment, our personal paths just so happening to crisscross as our planet spins around a star in an impossibly vast, ever-expanding, mind-bendingly mysterious universe. It's just all so wonderful and strange and beautiful and fascinating and—

"Earth to Captain Oblivious! Earth to Captain Oblivious!"

The voice barges into my brain and chases everything else out of it.

I blink—and realize that I've stopped halfway across the street, in the middle of a crosswalk, and that I'm blocking an SUV that's trying to make a turn.

"HELLO?!"

It's the driver of the car, his head sticking out of the window.

"You gonna move sometime this century, or what?!" he demands.

For half a second, I consider sharing with him what I'd been thinking—all that stuff about our crisscrossing paths and our strange, beautiful universe, and how we'd better not take it for granted, because you never know when it might, you know, *all of a sudden be reduced to dust*. But then the guy yanks his head back into his car and slams his hand down onto the horn.

BEEEEEEEEEEEEEEEEEEEEEEEEEEEEEEEP.

So I just hurry across the street and get on my way.

7.

I MANAGE TO MAKE IT ALL THE WAY HOME

without getting hit by a car or walking into a tree or doing anything else too Captain Oblivious–y.

Kitty's at the door waiting for me, tail wagging and tongue flapping. Probably because I'm late for his usual Saturday afternoon walk.

He's looking from me to his leash, which is dangling off one of the hooks of the nearby coatrack, his eyes bouncing back and forth like he's watching a fast-forwarded tennis match.

Me.

Leash.

Me.

Leash.

Me.

Leash.

Finally, I grab the leash and clip it to Kitty's collar.

He yelps with gratitude and excitement, leaps into the air, then rolls over onto his back and wriggles around like he's trying to scratch a terrible itch. He's not, really. It's just one of the many odd ways that the pooch expresses joy.

Watching him, a part of me envies Kitty—*his* obliviousness. I mean, the dog has never had a serious worry in his life. He exists within an impenetrable bubble of certainty that everything is okay and is going to go on being okay. It all sounds pretty darn nice.

But another part of me realizes that if we, the EngiNerds, really *can* do something about this threat to our planet . . . well, then we've got to do it. We can't just turn away, however daunting and terrifying it is. Deep down, I know that pretending everything is fine doesn't magically make everything fine. Ignoring a problem will never, ever fix it.

Kitty rolls over and climbs back up onto his feet, completing his we're-going-for-a-walk celebration. Then he yanks me out the door, across the porch, down the steps, and up the sidewalk, as eager as if he hasn't been outside in a week.

8.

IT FEELS LIKE KITTY AND I RUN AROUND

outside for *hours*.

Partly that's because I can't help but sneak glances up at the sky every thirty seconds or so. And there are plenty of clouds in it. But none of them ever appear to be sinking any lower. They're all stubbornly stuck up there in the atmosphere.

Still, my thoughts pick up speed every time I look at them. The concerns, the questions—they come at me *fast*.

Where's Dan?

What's he doing?

Is he scared?

Is he okay?

Will I ever see him again?

Should I have kept him from going up there?

Should I have at least asked the alien more questions before I let him go, like my parents used to ask me back when they first started letting me go out on bike rides by myself?

Like, where will you be going?

When will you be back?

Will you promise not to do anything dangerous or dumb?

And a couple other pretty important questions:

Why in the world is our planet in grave danger?

Who or what is about to annihilate it?

When Kitty and I finally get back home, I'm sure it's got to almost be dinnertime.

But when I step into the kitchen and check the clock, I find that a mere fifty-two minutes have passed.

Fifty. Two. Minutes.

Mikaela wasn't kidding when she said this was going to be the longest wait in history.

I head up to my bedroom and kill some time by making a list of things I could do to kill some time.

Then, one by one, I do them.

I inventory the shoeboxes of supplies that I keep on my shelves and in my closet.

I put away all the books and tools and toys that have gathered on my desk and piled up on my floor since I last put them away.

I clean out and organize my backpack, then refill every one of my mechanical pencils with lead and even replace all the erasers that need replacing.

 28

I'm just about to pull out my puzzle collection and count the pieces in each box to make sure none are missing when my mom calls me downstairs.

I head down to talk to her, for the first time in my life actually kind of hoping that she'll give me some chores to do.

She doesn't.

But she does something nearly as good.

She puts me in charge of ordering dinner.

So I sift through the stack of takeout menus we keep in the kitchen drawer and call in an epic order from General Noodles.

I hang around downstairs until the food arrives and engage my parents in a rousing game of Guess How Many Pairs of Chopsticks We'll Get With Our General Noodles Order.

Dad guesses two dozen.

Mom goes with *three* dozen.

I throw out an even fifty.

We're all wrong.

Our food arrives with *sixty-three* of the slim utensil-holding paper packages.

I'm pretty sure that's an all-time high.

We eat.

Midway through the meal, the phone rings. And even though I've managed, briefly, to distract myself from thinking about Dan, as soon as I hear that sound, my thoughts bounce right back to him, sucked there like a bunch of iron fillings to a magnet.

"I'll get it!" I shout.

And I'm out of my seat before my parents can even put down their chopsticks. I grab the phone and dart upstairs to my bedroom.

"Hello?"

"Remember the time John Henry Knox tried to tell that joke about the piece of rope?"

It's not Dan, but Jerry.

And apparently he called me up to . . . talk about something that happened—what was it—a year and a half ago?

"He couldn't get it out right," Jerry continues. "He kept doing it backward, saying the punch line before the setup. And Max found *that* so funny that he started cracking up, and he—he—"

Now it's *Jerry* who's cracking up. And Jerry's laugh? It's one of those infectious ones. Hearing it, you can't help but feel good—or at least a little better than you did before you heard it.

"He—he—"

Smiling, I finish for Jerry:

"He peed his pants."

Jerry erupts.

Which gets me laughing too.

"And then—" Jerry says, squeezing the words in between laughs where he can. "Then Amir—he—he said—"

"Oh yeah!" I laugh again, remembering. "He said *every time* he laughs he pees a couple drops."

"A couple drops!" Jerry shrieks.

I plop down onto my bed, sink my head into my pillow, and cast my mind back to that day. It was a good one. A great one, even. Our worries were microscopic. Maybe even nonexistent. We laughed and laughed. And it occurs to me then that *that's* what Jerry's up to. Offering some relief from this worrisome waiting for Dan. Which he knows might be most intense for me, his best and oldest friend.

Man.

Everyone deserves a friend as awesome as Jerry.

But he's not done yet.

Once he recovers from his latest bout of laughter, I hear a series of clicks and beeps. And then:

"You have reached the Knox Residence."

It's John Henry Knox, of course.

Jerry must've patched him in.

And even though John Henry Knox is most likely the most annoying know-it-all in human history, even though he possesses the astonishing capability to ruin every conversation he enters and I therefore try to strictly limit the amount of conversations I have with him . . . well, it's actually kind of nice to hear the kid's voice.

There's another bunch of beeps and clicks.

And a second later, Max is on the line.

Then Amir.

And Alan.

And Simon.

The only one of the EngiNerds that Jerry can't get on the phone is Edsley.

But he does finally reach Mikaela.

And since she wasn't there for John Henry Knox's first attempted telling of the rope joke, we ask him to give it another go.

Which somehow leads to even more laughter than it did the first time.

An hour later, when we all hang up, my throat aches and my eyes are still watering.

Have I forgotten about Dan?

Of course not.

Are my worries about him gone?

Not even slightly.

But thanks to my friends, I'm able to bear them a bit more easily.

Thanks to my friends, I'm even able, eventually, to close my eyes and get some sleep.

9.

I WAKE UP BRIGHT AND EARLY.

Or just *early*, since it's still not all that bright out yet.

It seems like the sun has just poked its head up into the sky, but it's hard to tell, what with all the clouds crowding the horizon.

I spend a couple minutes peering at the cottony puffs and tufts out of my bedroom window, desperate for answers about Dan.

Is he still up there?

Is he okay?

Are we going to be able to handle whatever this threat to our planet is?

Finally—and quietly, so I don't wake up Kitty and my parents—I head down to the kitchen.

There, I pluck a cookbook off the shelf and page through it until I locate the most complicated-looking breakfast recipe I can find.

Why?

Did I, in the middle of the night, decide that, should

the planet *not* be reduced to dust, I'm going to dedicate the rest of my life to perfecting the frittata or creating the world's greatest quiche?

Nope.

I just want to keep myself good and distracted until Dan finally arrives and fills me in on what the heck is going on.

But I don't even make it past the Table of Contents before I hear it:

Knock! Knock! Knock-knock knock!
Knock!
Knock!

It's Dan's knock.

The same one he always does and *has* done since the second grade.

I slam the cookbook shut and hurry for the door.

10.

"THANK GOD YOU'RE–" I SAY AS I SWING OPEN
the door.

"Here?" says Mikaela.

"You're not Dan."

She looks down at herself. Then back up at me.

"Correct," she confirms.

I glance behind her, at the clouds.

"How've you been holding up?" she asks.

"I was just about to cook my first frittata."

She snorts.

"Sounds about right," she says. "I reorganized my books. Twice. First chronologically, then by color."

"Dang," I tell her. "Wish I'd thought to do that."

Mikaela tips her head toward the rest of my house behind me.

"You want any help with that frittata?"

"I'd love some," I say, stepping back and opening the door up a little wider. "Come on in."

11.

IT TURNS OUT WE DON'T EVEN HAVE ALL THE
ingredients I'd need to make a proper frittata, so I fix a
couple bowls of cereal and Mikaela and I have breakfast
together.

"So . . . ," I say, sloshing my cereal around to get it a
little soggy. "I never really got a chance to say—"

"Don't," she stops me.

And I stop my spoon.

"Huh?"

"Apologize," Mikaela says. "Don't."

"Um," I say.

"Listen," she tells me. "I get it. Why you, you know . . ."

"Acted like a total jerk?" I offer.

"Right. You were confused. You were scared. You
were trying to protect your best friend."

I nod, because she's right.

"Still," I say, "I'm not sure that means I get to act like
a jerk."

"I guess not," she says.

I let go of my spoon.

Clear my throat.

And look Mikaela in the eye.

"I'm sorry," I tell her. "I doubted you. I thought the idea of aliens being responsible for everything that was going on was . . . crazy."

"And I get that," Mikaela says. "It's not exactly an easy thing to wrap your head around."

"Yeah, but I could've gone about struggling to wrap my head around it in a lot less jerky of a way. And you were *right*. And if you hadn't been there with us yesterday? Well . . ."

Mikaela grins.

"You would've been on the receiving end of a Klaus fart."

"Probably *more* than one. That was one ticked-off robot."

Mikaela laughs.

I do too.

And it feels good.

Though I can't help but also feel a tug of guilt for feeling good when I've *still* got no idea if Dan's all right. Especially since, at this point, he's been up there on that spaceship for over *twelve hours*. What could possibly be taking so long?

I grab my spoon and scoop up a bite of cereal. But then I set it right back down, because I realize I've got one more thing to say to Mikaela.

"Hey. I'm, uh—I'm glad you're *here*, too. For this." I wave my hand around. Up at the ceiling. Over toward the window above the sink, through which you can see a patch of cloudy sky. "Whatever *this* is."

Mikaela opens her mouth to answer.

But before she can:

Knock! Knock! Knock-knock-knock!
Knock!
Knock!

Mikaela grins again, then shoves her chair back and hops to her feet.

"Let's go find out."

12.

I SWING OPEN THE DOOR—

—and let out a long, low groan.

"Well," says John Henry Knox. "Good morning to you, *too*, Kennedy."

He leans to the side to see Mikaela.

"Hello, Mikaela."

Then he leans a little bit more to the side, a hopeful look on his face.

"Dan hasn't shown yet," I tell him.

John Henry Knox stands up straight—and sighs. His shoulders sink on the exhale. He looks like he's had a long, hard night.

"I couldn't sleep," he tells us. "I made a topographic map of my backyard. I taught myself conversational Portuguese. I read four graphic novels. Then I calculated how many chopsticks we'd need in order to build a ladder to the moon. And this morning, I made two batches of croissants. Also a frittata."

"A frittata?" I ask.

"Yes. The key is to use full-fat dairy, and to take the pan out of the oven just before the eggs are completely cooked."

I take a good long look at John Henry Knox.

At the dark bags beneath his tired eyes.

At the smear of egg yolk stuck to the back of his wrist.

And even though I know I might regret it, even though it'll probably only take five minutes for the kid to start to annoy me, I take a step back, open the door a little wider, and tell John Henry Knox, "Come on in."

13.

I'M WRONG:

It only takes *two* minutes for John Henry Knox to start to annoy me.

That's because, almost as soon as he takes a seat at my kitchen table, he starts spewing out a series of totally random, utterly useless facts.

For instance:

"Did you know that caterpillars have more muscles than humans?"

Or:

"Did you know that the average lead pencil can draw a line thirty-five miles long?"

Or:

"Did you know that it's against the law to fall asleep in a cheese factory in Illinois?"

It's after *this* one that Mikaela finally starts getting annoyed too.

"John Henry Knox," she says. "While the breadth and depth of your knowledge is truly astounding, this constant stream of facts is—"

"Slightly irritating?" he interrupts her to ask.

"Well . . . ," she says.

"It's okay," he assures her. "I've been told as much before. But one more fact is that, when I'm anxious, reciting trivia helps to keep me calm, and I am quite anxious to make sure that Dan has not been harmed and to find out what he has learned about the danger our planet is facing and if there is anything we can do to—"

Knock! Knock! Knock-knock knock!
Knock!
Knock!

My heart skips a beat.

But I tell myself not to get my hopes up.

Because the way today's going, it's not going to be Dan knocking at the door.

It's going to be Jerry.

Or Edsley.

Or, I don't know, someone who wants to talk to my parents first thing in the morning about how they can save forty-seven cents on their monthly energy bill by switching to a different provider.

But then whoever's knocking on the door goes and opens it on their own.

And a voice says, "Hello?"

It's a very familiar voice.

Dan's.

A beat later, he limps into the kitchen, a pained expression twisting up his face.

14.

MIKAELA GASPS AND LEAPS TO HER FEET.

"What happened?" she asks.

"Did the alien . . . ," says John Henry Knox, ". . . *hurt* you?"

I've got some questions too, but my heart's beating too erratically and my throat's too tight to possibly get a word out, much less a whole string of them. All I know is that I shouldn't have ever let Dan get on that spaceship. I should've stopped him. I should've protected him. What kind of best friend *am* I?

Dan looks at us for a moment, his face as serious as it's ever been.

Then he bursts out laughing.

I share a confused look with Mikaela and John Henry Knox.

"I'm fine," Dan says once he stops laughing. Then he hooks a thumb over his shoulder. "I tripped on the stairs out front and banged my shin."

Air comes rushing out of my lungs.

I guess I'd been holding my breath.

"Bem would never hurt me," Dan tells us.

"Bem?" asks John Henry Knox.

"That's his name?" Mikaela says.

Dan doesn't answer. Instead he waves me over to his side and throws an arm around my shoulders when I get there.

"I need something to eat," he says as I help him over to the table. "Also, like, ten thousand gallons of water. I've got a lot to tell you."

15.

WE LEAP INTO ACTION LIKE ONLY ENGINERDS

can.

John Henry Knox gathers some supplies from the fridge and then gets to work at the stove.

Mikaela finds a giant thermos and fills it with ice-cold water.

I grab a tube of antibiotic ointment and a few Band-Aids and help Dan cover up the scrape on his shin.

Just a few minutes after he limped through the doorway, Dan's bandaged up, thoroughly hydrated, and seated at the kitchen table with a plate of scrambled eggs and toast in front of him.

John Henry Knox forgot to get him a fork. But Dan's clearly as hungry as one of his robots. He just nudges some of the steam-spewing eggs onto one of the pieces of warm, buttery toast and scarfs it all down at a somewhat alarming speed.

Then he wipes his mouth.

Sits back.

Lets out a little burp.

And says:

"First of all, if any of you ever get a chance to go for a ride in a Plerpian spaceship, *take* it. That. Was. *Rad.*"

I don't know what "Plerpian" means, but hearing Dan say this, the last of the weight on my shoulders—all the worry and guilt I felt about letting him board that ship—drifts away.

But half a second later, the delight disappears from Dan's face, and a new kind of weight settles on me in the old one's place.

"Now," Dan says, "on to the other stuff . . ." He pauses to take a breath. "I guess I should start by telling you that our alien pal's name is Bempulthorpemckrackleflackin. But mostly what you need to understand is that it's all about the beans."

16.

"DID YOU JUST SAY *BUMBLE KRAKEN?*" I ASK.

"Did you just say *beans*?" asks Mikaela.

John Henry Knox says, "Did you need a fork?"

Dan answers him first. "I'm good," he says, and then begins fixing himself another piece of egg-topped toast. "And don't worry about the name. He said all his friends back home call him 'Bem.'"

"And where, exactly," I ask, "is *home*?"

Dan pauses with his second piece of toast a few inches from his mouth. He eyes each of us in turn, then says, "Bem's from a planet called Plerp-5, way over on the other side of the Milky Way." He lifts an eyebrow. "Do you all need a second?"

I nod, and then so do Mikaela and John Henry Knox.

Dan decimates his toast.

I watch him eat and replay his words in my head.

Bem.

Plerp-5.

Other side of the Milky Way.

It feels like my brain has been turned into a balloon and someone's pumping the poor thing full of way too much helium.

John Henry Knox, meanwhile, looks like he just got banged over the head with a frying pan.

And Mikaela?

She's just smiling. Probably because she's been so confident all along that there *was* extraterrestrial life out there in the universe, thriving on planets other than our own.

But her smile doesn't last long.

After just a handful of seconds, it flips over into a sort of determined frown.

"Okay," she says. "Now can we get back to the beans? And whatever it is they've got to do with our planet being reduced to dust in a couple weeks?"

17.

DID YOU KNOW THAT BEANS ARE PACKED

full of protein, fiber, vitamin B, iron, folate, calcium, potassium, phosphorous, and zinc? And did you know that they're also low in fat? Or what about the fact that all of this taken together means that eating lots of beans can help keep your blood and heart and lots of other important parts of your body healthy?

If you didn't know all this, don't worry.

Neither did I.

But John Henry Knox knew it (as he made sure to inform us).

And evidently, so have most of the rest of the life-forms existing in our galaxy.

Beans.

They're a big deal.

"Like, a *really* big deal," Dan tells us. "It's basically all they eat on Bem's planet, Plerp-5. And basically all they eat on Plerp-1, Plerp-2, Plerp-3, Plerp-4, Plerp-6, Plerp-7, Plerp-8, Plerp-10, Plerp-11, and Plerp-12, too."

"Wait a second," says Mikaela. "What happened to Plerp-9?"

Dan shakes his head.

"That's a whole separate story."

"Oh," Mikaela says.

"Anyway," Dan continues, "for years and years and years, Plerp-5 has been the main source of beans in the Plerpian System. Pretty much everyone on the planet is somehow involved in bean production, bean preparation, or bean packaging. There are the bean farmers, of course, and then the scientists who develop fertilizers and other stuff like that to help all the different varieties of beans grow as well as they possibly can. There are the engineers who make the machines that harvest the beans, and also the machines that help sort and ship the beans to the right factory. There are the factory workers, who perform quality control tests on the beans they get sent, and rinse and dry the bean varieties that need rinsing and drying, and then finally dump the things into cans or tubs or whatever other type of container they're supposed to be dumped into. And that's not even the half of it."

Dan stares down at his empty plate, like he was hoping another heap of hot eggs and a third piece of toast were going to have magically appeared. He presses some of the little leftover bread crumbs into his finger-tips, sprinkles them onto his tongue, and then goes on.

"There are the Plerpians who run the companies that sell the beans, and all the employees there who

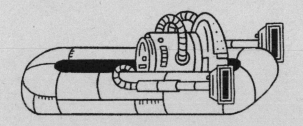

help do what it takes to run a whole big bean company. There are the designers and artists who make the logos that go on the cans and tubs and other containers of beans, and the musicians who make the songs that they play on the commercials to advertise them, and the—"

"Okay," I say, stopping Dan before he can start tell-ing us about the team of Plerpians who make the glue that they use to fix the labels to the cans and tubs and containers of beans, or the individual actors who play the happy bean-eating Plerpian family in the commer-cials in which the Plerpian musicians' songs play.

I'm beginning to see why it took Bem all night to explain things to Dan.

"We get it," I say. "It's all beans all the time over on Plerp-5. The whole planet runs on the things. What's that got to do with *us*?"

"Well, that's the thing," says Dan. "The whole planet ran on beans—until recently. . . ."

18.

I WON'T MAKE YOU SIT THROUGH DAN'S whole long explanation of the economic woes of Plerp-5. Instead, I'll just tell you what you need to know:

A few years ago, the Plerpians on Plerp-12 got sick and tired of the Plerpians on Plerp-5 running the bean show. (Not *The Bean Show*, which, Dan shared, is a long-running variety show produced by a team of Plerpians on Plerp-7. Apparently Plerpians from *all* the planets in the Plerpian System agree that *The Bean Show* is totally wonderful, and nothing should be done to mess with it.) Anyway, the sick and tired Plerpians on Plerp-12 began playing around with producing beans on *their* planet. It took some time, but evidently Plerp-12 developed a sort of super bean—at least that's what they're *calling it* in all their advertisements. And whether or not it's true (Bem, for what it's worth, is fairly certain it's *not*), the rest of the Plerpians in the Plerpian System are buying it. *Literally.* Sales of Plerp-5 beans have totally tanked. And so the Planetary

Leadership of Plerp-5 has decided to launch a little advertising campaign of their own.

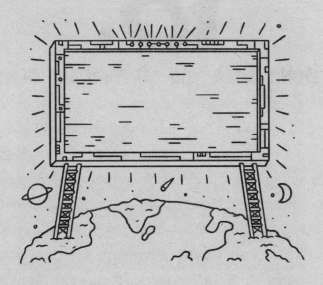

"It's wild," Dan says. "The Plerpians on Plerp-5—they've developed these crazy new billboards. They're gigantic. Enormous. Humongous. They're—they're *ginormongous*. Some of them are, no joke, the size of a planet. They light up and glow and even beam and project, and they've got this positioning technology they use that means if they put them in certain spots the things can be seen from, like, light-years away. It's pretty astounding."

"Sounds cool," Mikaela says. "But I'm still not—"

She stops midsentence.

And her eyes go wide.

Like, *scarily* wide.

"What?" John Henry Knox asks her. "I don't—"

Now *his* eyes go wide.

And he says:

"Oh. *Oh no.*"

19.

"ALL RIGHT," I SAY. "IF SOMEONE DOESN'T
clue me in as to how in the world all this nonsense about
beans and *ginormongous billboards* is related to our
planet being reduced to dust in the frighteningly near
future, I may just lose my mind."

Dan looks at me, and then over at Mikaela.

Then they both turn their heads toward John Henry
Knox.

"What?" I say, growing increasingly frustrated that I
haven't figured it out yet.

"The billboards . . . ," Dan says. "They have to be
placed in particular, very specific locations in order to
be seen from far away . . ."

"You said that already," I tell him, *still* not getting it.

"And," Mikaela adds, "he said that some of the billboards are as big as *planets. . . .*"

"And I heard him," I say. "But what does that—"

It's then, at last, that it clicks.

"Oh."

I sit there with the realization for a minute. It's a lot to take in, especially on top of all the *other* stuff I've had to take in over the course of the last twenty-four hours or so. And once I've finally begun to wrap my head around it, I ask Dan, just to make sure I'm right.

"Our planet . . . ," I say. "Earth . . . It's—it's one of those locations?"

Dan gulps.

And nods his head.

20.

MY HEAD'S SPINNING LIKE A MERRY-GO-ROUND

moving at warp speed. My heart's thrumming like a possessed jackhammer.

I'm on my feet.

Pacing back and forth across the kitchen.

Kind of—

Scratch that.

—*definitely* freaking out.

"So they're just gonna *destroy* our planet so they can put up a *billboard*?" I say. "That's—that's *ludicrous*. That's *absurd*. It—it should be *illegal*. I mean, don't these Plerpians have *laws*? Isn't there some kind of rule about not reducing a planet with nearly eight billion self-conscious life-forms and thousands of years of recorded history into dust just to save your *bean business*?!"

"Well," says Dan, "that's sort of the problem."

I stop my pacing.

"What is?"

"Us," he says. "And our history. The most recent bits of it, at least."

I go back to the table.

Take a seat.

And lean in nice and close to Dan.

"WHAT?!"

Dan scoots his chair back.

Wipes the spit I accidentally deposited on him off of his face.

Takes a deep breath.

And explains . . .

21.

"THE PLERPIANS OF PLERP-5 IDENTIFIED OUR

planet as an ideal location for one of their billboards
about three months ago," Dan says. "Ever since then,
they've been keeping an eye on us, exhaustively studying our ways. They've been sending ships, disguised as
clouds, for the past several weeks, and consuming as
much of our culture as they can. Because, sure, they're
desperate to get these billboards up. But they're not, as
you said, Ken, going to annihilate a planet with nearly
eight billion self-conscious life-forms and thousands of
years of recorded history just to do it."

"Oh-*kay* . . . ," I say. "Then I really don't see what the
problem is."

"The *problem*," says Dan, "is that we've done a darn
good job convincing the Plerpians that we're just a bunch
of selfish, careless, destructive idiots, and that we don't
actually care much for *our* planet or anyone else's, either."

I look around the table, at Mikaela and John Henry
Knox.

"No," says Dan. "Not, like, us *specifically*. I mean the collective *we*. Humanity as a whole."

I turn back to Dan.

"Continue . . . ," I say.

"At first, the Plerpians assumed that we were getting ready to abandon our planet and take up residence on a brand-new one. That was the only way they could make sense of our behavior, so much of which is actively *damaging* our planet, making it increasingly less habitable for ourselves and most other living things by the day. But when they couldn't find any indication that *that* was true, they were forced to conclude—"

"That we're a bunch of selfish, careless, destructive idiots," Mikaela interrupts.

"And that we're on the verge of annihilating our planet anyway," adds John Henry Knox.

"Exactly," says Dan. He winces. "But then it sorta gets a little bit worse. . . ."

"*Worse?!*" I say. "How can it possibly get any *worse*?"

"Well," he says, "some of the Plerpian scientists are under the impression that if we're allowed to continue in our selfish, careless, destructive, idiotic ways, we'll not only destroy our own planet but potentially start doing damage to our solar system, and maybe, eventually, even the galaxy as a whole."

"Okay," I say, slumping in my chair. "I guess *that's* how it gets worse."

"We're like the ultimate bad neighbors," Dan says. "So for the Planetary Leaders of Plerp-5, it's kind of a win-win. They get to feel good about knocking a dangerous species out of the galaxy, plus they get to build their billboard and try to save their bean business."

And then Dan's silent.

We all are.

Because here's the thing:

The Plerpians—they're not wrong.

Humans haven't been doing all that great of a job taking care of our planet. We have, in fact, been doing a *terrible* job of it. And even though the four of us sitting at that table haven't been the ones making the big decisions that are most responsible for the damage being done to the planet—well, in this situation, it doesn't matter. Because as far as the Planetary Leadership of Plerp-5 is concerned, it seems, we're all responsible. And maybe that's sort of true. Maybe all the rest of us haven't been doing enough to *stop* the decision-makers from making those big, terrible decisions.

The silence stretches on.

And on.

And I'm pretty sure it might just go on stretching until my house and kitchen and the chairs under our butts all get reduced to dust along with the rest of the world.

But then Kitty lets out a wobbly moan from somewhere else in the house.

And I know the pup's probably still asleep, dreaming about rolling around in a heap of leftover pieces of pizza or diving into a massive muddy puddle. But I can't help but think that maybe Kitty's been listening in on our conversation, and that that wobbly moan is an expression of how he feels.

Because that's pretty much exactly how I feel.

Like moaning.

And then maybe crying for a bit.

And then maybe curling up into a little ball and—

"Hang on," I say, my mood lifting a little just before it hits rock bottom. "Bcm said he came down here to help us. To try to help *save us again*. So he's got to have a *plan*, right?"

Dan doesn't answer.

"Right?!"

22.

BEM *DOESN'T* HAVE A PLAN.

"He *did* help, though," Dan says, coming to the alien's defense. "And he still is."

Reaching into his pocket, Dan pulls out a slim, rectangular object. Its dulled silver color makes me think, for a split second, that it's one of the duct tape wallets Dan and I made a couple years back. But then I see that the thing's got a screen. The screen's got a spiderweb's worth of cracks running through it, but when Dan swipes it with his thumb, it illuminates with a soft, greenish glow.

I can sense the excitement building in Mikaela from all the way across the table.

"Is that . . . ," she says, "*a Plerpian communication device?!*"

"An old one," Dan says, passing the gadget to Mikaela. She takes it gingerly, handling it like it's a ticking time bomb or an enormous diamond. "Bem said it's a bit fritzy, and sometimes gets spammed. Apparently he keeps asking his parents for a nicer model, but he just keeps getting his siblings' hand-me-downs. But he's got one too. So as long as this one doesn't fall apart on us, we can talk to him, even though he's got to stay up there." He points at the ceiling.

"Oh, excellent," I say, not seeing how this is even remotely helpful. "So he can give us a play-by-play AS OUR PLANET IS REDUCED TO DUST?!"

"Being able to communicate with him could prove extremely useful," Dan argues. "Also"—he sets a greenish-gray, pocket-size book on the table—"he gave us this."

John Henry Knox plucks the book up and reads us the title. *"Plerpian Protocols for Planetary Demolition. Eleventh Edition. English Translation."* Opening to a random page, narrowing his eyes at the incredibly tiny font, he reads, "'Protocol #2,027: No species of legume may be harmed in the course of the demolition of a planet. If a heretofore unknown species of legume is discovered during the course of the demolition of a planet, said legume must be carefully extracted, removed from danger, and properly preserved for later study before demolition may recommence.'"

"Wonderful," I say, pretty sure this is even *less* helpful

than a busted communication device. "Glad we've got some riveting new reading material to enjoy AS OUR PLANET IS REDUCED TO DUST. You're the best, *Bem*."

"It's only because of Bem that we even know our planet is under threat," Dan says. "If not for him, a week or two from now, it'd just be . . . you know, not pretty."

"To say the least," says John Henry Knox.

"Bem's up there poring over these protocols, trying to find some sort of loophole, anything to delay the demolition crew. Hopefully permanently. And thanks to the communication device," Dan continues, "he can give us a heads-up about anything else we need to know. Also . . ."

I'd been looking at the communication device in Mikaela's hands—but hearing Dan trail off, registering the sudden absence of confidence in his voice, I look back up at him. He's studying the crumbs on his plate like somehow *they* might be the key to saving our planet.

"Dan . . . ," I say, knowing he's got something else to say, knowing he's worried about how we might react to it.

Clearing his throat, keeping his eyes down on those crumbs, Dan says, "Bem also . . . well . . . he convinced the Planetary Leadership of Plerp-5 to have the demolition crew begin their work in our town."

John Henry Knox lets out a strangled hiccup and drops the eleventh edition of the *Plerpian Protocols for Planetary Demolition*. It looks like his frittata's about to make a reappearance on my kitchen table.

I swing back toward Dan. "How . . . ," I ask him, through clenched teeth, ". . . is *that* . . . HELPFUL?!"

"He believes in us," Mikaela says, sounding impossibly, infuriatingly calm. "He thinks we can figure out how to stop all this."

Dan nods.

"He said we're humanity's best hope."

"We're—" I sputter. "We're kids! That's all. We're—we're a bunch of KIDS!"

"Plerpians believe that the younger a mind is, the more flexible it can be, the more creative and innovative its ideas can be. That's why Bem's here in the first place," Dan says. "It's his job. He's a 'scout.' Even though he's a kid, he was tasked with finding the best place to start methodically demolishing our planet. Even though he's a kid, he was given his very own spaceship, and is allowed to fly it around all by himself."

"Great," I say. "Sooooooo helpfu—"

My sarcasm is cut short by the sight of something in the window above the sink. It's a cloud. But, as I've become intensely aware, not all the clouds looming over us are *just* clouds. What's more, this is a big ol' cumulonimbus cloud, one whose puffs and peaks roughly form the shape of a UFO. It stands out sharply against the rest of the early-morning clouds in the sky, as it's clearly closer to the ground, and every second sinking *more* closely toward it in a very unnatural, not cloudlike way.

"I thought you said Bem couldn't come back down here . . . ," I say.

"What?" says Dan, twisting around in his chair to look out the window, too.

Beep-beep BOOP.

Mikaela jumps in her seat and drops the communication device, which continues to *beep* and *BOOP* on the table.

Dan snatches the device up and turns it over to see the screen.

His eyes grow about a dozen sizes.

"Um," he says. "That's not *Bem's* ship . . . Apparently the demolition crew has decided to get a bit of a head start on their work."

23.

TWO SECONDS LATER. WE'RE ALL ON OUR feet.

Scrambling for the window.

Knocking into one another.

Just generally *freaking out* and making all sorts of noise.

We're loud enough to wake up Kitty, who barrels into the room and starts barking like crazy despite the fact that he's got no clue what's going on.

And Kitty—well, *he's* loud enough to wake up my parents.

I can hear them fumbling around upstairs. And then, a second later:

"Kitty! Kitty—SHHH!"

It's my dad, hissing down the stairs to try to get Kitty to quit making a racket.

But trying to calm down Kitty once he's got himself good and riled up is about as easy as stopping a meteor that's just pierced our atmosphere from racing toward the ground. Really, there's no point in even trying. The best course of action is to just *get out of the way*.

Meanwhile, the four of us—me, Dan, Mikaela, and John Henry Knox—are squeezed around the sink, craning our necks to better see out the window as that massive, UFO-shaped cumulonimbus sinks lower and lower toward the ground.

Just as it slips out of sight beneath the tops of the trees in my backyard, I hear my dad behind me.

"Ken?"

I turn, as do Dan and Mikaela and John Henry Knox, and see my dad in the kitchen doorway, his eyes bleary and his hair sticking up in about seventeen thousand different directions.

Oh, also, he's wearing nothing but his underwear.

He leaps back through the doorway and around the corner as soon as the realization that I'm not alone lands in his sleep-foggy brain. There, safely out of sight, he calls out:

"Um. Hi! Hey! Good—good morning, everyone. Didn't, ah, know you had friends over, Ken. Is—is everything all right down here?"

I glance back toward the window.

Still no cloud.

Meaning, of course, that everything is absolutely *not* all right down here.

But I'm not about to tell my dad what's really going on.

Well, maybe I *will* have to tell him sooner or later—but I'm certainly not going to do it before the poor guy's had his morning coffee and gotten some clothes on.

So I just say:

"Yep! Kitty's ready for his morning walk. That's all."

Then I add:

"You can go back to bed."

"Right," says Dad. "Ah, yeah. I'll—I'll, ah, do that. See you kids later. Have fun!"

Dad heads back upstairs.

And as soon as he's gone, I dart across the kitchen and over to the door.

I tug it open, then turn to Dan and Mikaela and John Henry Knox.

"Ready to track down a spaceship?" I ask them, hoping they say yes, because I'm not feeling so prepared myself.

But before they can answer, Kitty launches himself

out the open door and down the porch steps. Two seconds later, he's tearing up the street.

"*He* sure is," says John Henry Knox.

"If only," I say.

Then I rush out into the street after him.

24.

WE RUN.

We run like chickens with their heads cut off.

Or, no:

We run like a bunch of kids who know that their whole entire world might be reduced to a bunch of cosmic dust bunnies in a matter of minutes.

Kitty, meanwhile, runs like he always does. He lopes along with his tongue lolling out of his mouth and a big stupid grin on his face, like it's the gosh-darn greatest day EVER and he doesn't have a care in the world.

Which, I suppose, he doesn't.

Man.

Whoever came up with that expression "ignorance is bliss" should probably be given some sort of genius award.

Speaking of genius?

We aren't exhibiting any of it.

I'm just following Kitty, because as much as we really need to locate that cloud, we also really, really,

really can't afford to lose sight of the pooch. Left to his own devices, he's capable of causing nearly as much trouble as Mike Edsley. And I guess because I appear to be running with some sort of purpose, Dan and Mikaela and John Henry Knox are following me.

Finally, after chasing Kitty for four or five blocks, I manage to charge up alongside him and, by angling my steps, force him over onto someone's lawn. As soon as he hops off the pavement and onto the grass, I dive. I get my arms around his middle, scoop him against my chest, and together we roll to a stop.

As soon as we do, I throw my head back and search the sky.

There are plenty of clouds up there—but not *the* cloud.

My stomach twists into a ball of knots.

Not because I'm the least bit looking forward to facing a Plerpian demolition crew, but because, as the only people on the planet who know what's going on, I know that my friends and I might be the only ones equipped to *stop* them.

"We need to split up," Mikaela says. "We'll cover more ground that way."

I nod, since I'm too out of breath to answer.

Dan and John Henry Knox do the same.

"I'll go north," says Mikaela. "Dan—you head east. John Henry Knox—you can take west. And Ken, you—"

Just then, elsewhere in the neighborhood, a dog starts to bark.

And Kitty instantly becomes *Super Kitty* and uses his super strength to wriggle out of my arms and rush off in the direction of the commotion.

"Okay," Mikaela says. "Ken—I guess *you* should go west."

25.

FORTUNATELY, THE BARKING DOG THAT KITTY

just *has* to go and find is only a few blocks away.

*Un*fortunately, the dog is barking because an enormous, UFO-shaped cumulonimbus cloud is sitting in the street, interrupting the pup's morning walk and, most likely, *freaking it out.*

Also freaked out?

The dog's owner.

He's young-looking, like maybe he only just graduated from college. But I don't think anything he learned *there* could've possibly prepared him for *this.*

After a couple seconds, he notices me standing nearby. He turns to face me, his eyes big and unblinking, his jaw hanging down as far as it goes.

"Wha—whaaaa?" he says, lifting a hand and aiming a shaky finger at the cloud.

I turn toward it—and make a split-second decision.

"What?" I say, turning back to the guy, as nonchalantly as I can.

And now he's giving me the same wide-eyed, jaw-dropped look he was giving the cloud a moment ago.

"The—" he says. "The *cloud*. The one your dog is running laps around."

I look again.

Then say:

"What cloud?"

"You—you don't see it?" he asks me.

"See what?" I say.

The guy drops his dog's leash and holds on to either side of his head, like he's worried his brain might burst.

Do I feel bad about making this guy feel crazy?

Yeah, a little bit.

But I'm willing to bet he'll feel even *crazier* when the puffs of that cumulonimbus cloud part, revealing a metal door, and a ramp—*and an alien demolition crew*.

My hope is to make the guy feel like he's dreaming, and to get him going on his way.

So I start spewing some totally random—but I guess not *utterly* useless—facts that I just learned that morning:

"Caterpillars have more muscles than humans."

The guy gulps.

"Wha-wha-what?" he stammers.

"The average lead pencil can draw a line thirty-five miles long."

The guy takes a step back, away from me.

And I take a step toward him.

"It's against the law to fall asleep in a cheese factory in Illinois."

That does it.

The guy scoops up his dog and hurries off.

I turn back to the cloud just in time to see Kitty, still running laps around the thing, streak by.

A second later, a ramp pokes out of one of the cloud's curled, thinning puffs and reaches for the ground like a long metallic tongue.

I take a shaky breath.

Ready or not—and, yeah, I'm *not*—here they come . . .

26.

I STAND THERE AND WATCH THE SPACESHIP'S
ramp meet the pavement with a soft *click*.

"*Kitty,*" I whisper-shout as authoritatively as I can.

The pooch is still running laps around the ship, and I have this horrible vision of the otherworldly demolition crew stepping out onto the ramp, getting spooked by the big, furry blur circling their vehicle, and, well, doing something or other to *demolish* it.

I try again, a bit more forcefully:

"*KITTY! COME! HERE!*"

But this backfires.

Hearing his name only gets the pup even more excited, and now he's not just running laps around the ship, he's running laps around the ship *and* barking his head off.

I quickly scan the ground around me for a rock. Because Kitty *loves* rocks. The bigger the better. He'll lick the things for hours on end, like he thinks that sooner or later, if he just keeps it up, he'll reach some sort of pizza-stuffed center.

But before I can find anything to entice the dog, I notice a figure emerge from the ship. The alien stops at the top of the ramp to take a look around, and I just go on standing there, rigid with fear.

I wince as Kitty comes barreling around the corner once more.

But the alien . . .

Well, if anything, he seems delighted to see the dog.

For a moment, he just watches Kitty, the excitement building on his face.

Then the alien calls back into his ship:

"Muckle, come quick! There is a pupperoni out here."

27.

I CAN SEE THE ALIEN'S UNDERPANTS.

That's something you should probably know.

He's bigger than Bem—about the size of an average adult human—and is wearing a collared button-down shirt, a bright striped tie, and a pair of blindingly white underpants. Which I can see since he's not wearing any *pants* pants. Which, along with my dad, makes the alien the second creature whose underwear I've seen today. And it's not even seven o'clock in the morning yet.

What a day.

"Muckle," the alien calls back into the ship. "Hurry. You must witness the speed and grace of this majestic creature."

"I am coming as fast as I am able, Kermin," comes a second voice from inside the ship. "I fear I may have misplaced my zap-cannon."

"I have not misplaced my zap-cannon. I have safely stored it beneath the elastic band of my human under-garments. We may take turns employing mine, if you—"

The alien stops talking because Kitty has all of a sudden stopped running. He plops himself down on one of the nearby lawns, panting furiously, and kicks his back leg up toward his head to scratch an itch behind his ear.

"Muckle! Muckle!" the alien on the ramp shouts. "The pupperoni! He is flexible! Extraordinarily flexib—"

This time, the alien stops talking because Kitty, having scratched his itch, has come trotting over to my side.

Which, of course, has caused the alien to finally notice *me*, still standing right where I have been all along, as stiff as a steel rod—a very, very frightened steel rod.

And based on the way the alien's expression immediately darkens at the sight of me, I can tell he's not as big a fan of human beings as he is of dogs.

28.

A MOMENT AFTER THE FIRST ALIEN FINALLY
notices me, the second steps out onto the ramp behind
him. He's roughly the same size as the other and dressed
similarly—in a collared button-down shirt and a bright
striped tie. And, yeah, he's also got that whole underpants but no *pants* pants thing going on.

"Kermin," he says to his partner. "You did not inform
me the pupperoni was accompanied by a human."

"I realize, Muckle," says the first alien, whose name,
I guess, is Kermin. "I have only now discovered the
human."

Together, the aliens eye me.

I let them, standing as still as I can, heart pound-
ing, sweat forming on my brow, worried that if I make
any sudden movements, Kermin might pull out his zap-
cannon thingamajig and use it on me.

After what seems like an hour, but really must be
only a couple seconds, Kermin takes a step down the
ramp, closer to me.

"Careful, Kermin," says the other alien, who evidently goes by the name Muckle. "Recall that Chief Scientist Fliffersnapper could not determine whether or not human beings' stupidity is contagious."

"I recall," Kermin says. "But the pupperoni is in very close proximity to the human and its stupidity, and he does not appear to have been infected. The pupperoni appears to be as observant and insightful as ever."

Without moving my head, I aim my eyes down at Kitty. He's just sitting there beside me, breathing hard, his slobbery tongue drooping goofily out of his mouth.

"I suppose you are correct, Kermin," says Muckle.

At which point Kermin takes another step down the ramp.

Followed by another.

And then a few more, the fear in my body building with each one.

The alien pauses there before taking

one last step, which brings him off the ramp and onto the pavement of the street. He's now just a few yards away from me, and once Muckle, still up at the top of the ramp, sees that his pal hasn't fallen down in a fit of human-induced idiocy, he comes down and joins him.

"GREET-TINGS, HUE-MAN," Kermin calls to me, separating every syllable and taking it nice and slow. "I AM KER-MIN-FLAP-PER. THIS IS MY AH-SOSH-EE-IT MUCK-ULL-MICK-DUNK."

"YOUR PLAN-ET," Muckle shouts in a similar fashion, "IS BOTH FASS-SIN-ATE-ING AND BE-YOU-TIFF-ULL."

My eyes go wide, and I feel a hint of hope stir in my stomach.

Because if these aliens find our planet fascinating and beautiful, maybe they've changed their minds about demolishing it and just haven't informed Bem yet.

"Wow," I say, taking it slow myself, worried about possibly saying the wrong thing. "Uh, thanks. And, yeah—I mean, I agree."

I look around. First at the little tree standing in the middle of one of the nearby lawns, its branches criss-crossing and creating diamond patterns against the sky. Then at the bush that sits at the tree's base, studded with bright red berries and awash with movement from a gentle breeze. And then at the grass-covered ground around it all, beneath which, I know, curl and twist an incredible nervous system–like network of powerful roots.

"It really *is* fascinating and beautiful," I say, turning back to the aliens. "I'm glad you think so."

"YES," shouts Kermin. "THINK SO WE DO."

And then Muckle says, "WE WILL NOW PRO-SEED TO METH-OD-IC-AL-LEE DEE-MOLL-ISH IT."

29.

KERMIN LIFTS HIS HAND AND AIMS A THIN

silver cylinder at the bush whose fascinating beauty I'd just been admiring, and a split second later—well, it's gone.

Like, *gone* gone.

Like, it's no longer there.

Like, it's just been, in the literal blink of an eye, wiped out of earthly existence.

In the bush's place sits a small pile of greenish-brown dust, the size and shape of an anthill.

This is, without a doubt, the most bafflingly terrifying thing I have ever seen—and remember, just yesterday I was dodging the superfast farts of an extremely angry robot. But that's *nothing* compared to this. I've reached a brand-new level of terror. My brain feels like it's tumbling down a never-ending mountain, and I'm all of a sudden shivering and sweating at the same time. I want to run. I really, *really* want to run. But I'm also intensely aware that running won't accomplish anything—besides maybe getting me turned into a pile of dust faster than I might otherwise be turned into one, that is.

I turn back to the aliens just in time to see Muckle reach for the silver cylinder in his associate's hand.

My brain fills with noise, like someone just cranked up the volume knob on my thoughts.

No no no no please No please NO PLEASE—

Kermin pulls the weapon away before Muckle can grab it.

"Kermin," Muckle says. "You claimed we could take turns employing your zap-cannon."

"I recall, Muckle," says Kermin. "But my turn has not yet expired. I am allowed multiple zaps per turn. I am allowed . . . *four* zaps."

Muckle glares at Kermin.

"You have just invented this rule," he claims. "That is not reasonable."

Kermin lifts his chin. "You may employ your own zap-cannon, then."

"I have previously informed you, Kermin, that I have misplaced my zap-cannon."

"And I ask you, Muckle—was that my failing? I believe not. Now, if you are able to pardon me, I have a planet to methodically demolish."

Kermin aims the silver cylinder at the tree, the one that had only seconds ago had a beautiful, fascinating bush at its base.

And I know I need to hurry up and *do* something.

Unfortunately, my terror seems to have transformed me back into a sweat-drenched steel rod.

But luckily for me—and for the rest of the planet, too—I don't end up *having* to do anything.

For now, at least.

Because before the alien can reduce anything else to dust, Kitty throws his head back and lets out a loud, commanding bark.

30.

KERMIN LOWERS THE ZAP-CANNON AND

turns to Kitty.

"The pupperoni," he says to Muckle. "It would appear he wishes to speak."

As if to confirm this, Kitty lets out a whole round of barks.

"Rarf! Rarf! Rarf! Rarf!"

Kermin angles his head, tipping his ear so it's aimed directly at Kitty.

"Please, pupperoni," the alien says. "Proceed."

Kitty once again barks:

"Rarf! Rarf-rarf RARF!"

Kermin, meanwhile, has his face scrunched up in concentration.

"Kermin," Muckle says after a moment. "I ask you to recall that Chief Scientist Fliffersnapper was unable to decipher the complicated language of the pupperoni."

Kermin's face falls into a frown.

But only for a second.

Then he's turning to me, hope brightening his big, otherworldly eyes.

"HUE-MAN," Kermin calls to me.

"Uhh," I say. "Yes?"

"I UNDERSTAND THAT YOUR SPECIES HAS A VERY LIMITED MENTAL CAPACITY. THAT, DESPITE HAVING RATHER LARGE BRAINS IN YOUR SKULLS, YOU EMPLOY ONLY A VERY SMALL FRACTION OF THEIR POWER, AND TYPI-CALLY DO SO FOR INANE, SELF-DESTRUCTIVE PURPOSES. HOWEVER, YOUR SPECIES HAS EXHIBITED A SMALL AMOUNT OF CLEAR THINKING AND SENSE BY DECIDING TO SUR-ROUND YOURSELVES AND POPULATE YOUR PLANET WITH SEVERAL VASTLY SUPERIOR SPE-CIES. AN EXAMPLE: CANINES."

Here Kermin pauses to point—and smile—at Kitty.

Kitty says:

"RARF!"

"I ASK YOU," Kermin says, addressing me again. "IS IT POSSIBLE THAT YOU, DUE TO EXTEN-SIVE AMOUNTS OF EXPOSURE AS OPPOSED TO ANY INNATE OR ACQUIRED COGNITIVE ABILI-TIES, HAVE BECOME ABLE TO COMPREHEND

THE PUPPERONI TONGUE AND CAN RELAY THE MEANING OF HIS *RARF*S TO US?"

It takes me a minute to pick all this apart.

But I'm pretty sure the alien is saying something along the lines of this:

I know you're super stupid, just like all the rest of humanity. But clearly you're not SO stupid that you can't see how awesome dogs are. Is there any chance that, since you've spent a lot of time with dogs, you can understand their language and can translate it for us?

Once I've got all this straight in my head, I look down at Kitty, and he looks up at me.

And I wonder . . .

Could he be as brilliant as these aliens seem to think he is?

As much as I love him—and I love Kitty as much as anything or any*one* on the planet—I've always thought of the pooch as having, well, a particularly "limited mental capacity."

But am *I* the dumb one?

Is it just that I can't fathom Kitty's intelligence?

"Kermin," I hear Muckle say. "It appears the human has fallen asleep. Your query must have overtaxed and exhausted his brain."

."Negative," Kermin says. "His eyelids remain flapping. We must allow time for his inferior brain to process my request."

"Kitty," I say. Quietly. So only he can hear. "I don't know if you understand what I'm saying. But if you do, I could really use your help here. Get us out of this, and I'll never stop you from licking the kitchen floor again. I'll never—"

"HUE-MAN!" Muckle shouts. "CEASE! SLEEPING!"

I give Kitty one last pleading look, then lift my head.

"Yeah," I tell the aliens. "I can, uh, relay the meaning of his *rarf*s to you."

Kermin grins.

Then says:

"Excellent."

31.

WHETHER OR NOT KITTY IS ACTUALLY AS

smart as the Plerpians seem to believe he is, whether or not he truly understands what it is I'm asking him to do, I don't know.

All I know is that he does it *beautifully*.

He barks in all the right places and does so with enough tonal variety that it really does sound like he's speaking a complicated language instead of just, you know, barking over and over again. And after every "phrase" he "speaks," he waits until I'm done "translating" before he starts up again, like he gets exactly what I'm up to. The pooch even throws in a few dramatic pauses to *really* sell it.

It's either the greatest, most statistically unlikely series of coincidences in the history of human and canine relationships, or the dog's a downright genius.

"Rarf!" Kitty says.

And I translate for the aliens, whose eyes ping-pong back and forth between Kitty and me the entire time:

"Thank you for allowing me an opportunity to speak."

"Ruff-ruff RARF-rarf!" Kitty says.

And I translate:

"Welcome to the planet Earth."

We go back and forth nearly a dozen times.

Kitty:

"Ruff RUFF-ruff rarf ruff!"

Me:

"I understand you are here on some very important demolition business."

Kitty:

"RARF ruuuuuuuff?"

Me:

"But may I please request a favor of you?"

Kitty:

"Ruff-ruff-ruff! Ruff-ruff-ruff! Ruff-ruff-ruff ruff RUFF!"

Me:

"We, uh . . . um . . . we have a very important . . . *dog meeting* tomorrow morning. Yes. A . . . big dog meeting. A canine conference at, uh . . . at the one and only Feldman's Field."

Kitty:

"Rarf-ruff raaaaaaaarf!"

Me:

"So if you could maybe refrain from demolishing our planet for a little bit longer . . ."

Kitty:

"Ruff-ruff rarf-rarf! Ruff RARF-RARF-RARF!"

Me:

". . . that'd be super hugely appreciated."

Kitty:

"RUFF-RUFF rarf!"

Me:

"Thank you for considering this request."

Kitty:

"Ruff-ruff-ruff-ruff RARF-rarf!"

Me:

"You . . . magnanimous creatures, you."

Kitty:

"RARF!"

Me:

"Okay. I'm done speaking now."

Kermin is grinning.

Muckle looks slightly suspicious.

Which is worrisome.

But he's not the one who makes the final decision.

"YES!" shouts Kermin. "We enthusiastically agree to the pupperoni's request!"

My heart slows.

My lungs loosen.

My shoulders sink.

"We shall refrain from methodically demolishing the remainder of your planet until tomorrow's morning has ceased," Kermin goes on. "Demolition will recommence tomorrow at the time you refer to as *noon*."

The alien continues grinning at Kitty for a moment, then directs his attention toward me.

"It is conceivable," he says, "that you are not as stupid and useless as you seem to be, human."

"Uhh," I say. "Thanks?"

And then, just like that, the aliens turn around, climb their ramp, and disappear back into their spaceship.

32.

KITTY AND I REMAIN RIGHT WHERE WE ARE

as the door of the spaceship closes and is quickly covered up by a swirl of cloud. Seconds later, I can no longer make out any of the ship's charcoal-colored hull. And then, as quietly as the movements of an actual mass of condensed water vapor, the cloud-draped spaceship lifts off the ground and rises into the air.

I feel some of my fear drift up and away with it.

Kitty lifts his head and licks the tips of my fingers, as if he's comforting me, telling me I can relax.

I tip my head back to follow the spaceship up into the sky. And just about when it's fully camouflaged among all the real clouds up there, I hear:

"Ken!"

It's Dan, hurrying up the street toward me.

Mikaela and John Henry Knox aren't far behind.

"Was that the ship?" Dan says, pointing up at the clouds. "I thought I saw it going back up. Did you see the dem—" He gets tripped up on the word. "The demolition crew?"

I nod.

Dan, Mikaela, and John Henry Knox peer into the sky to try to see where the ship has gone.

"What—what happened?" Dan finally asks.

I look down at Kitty.

The dog's staring up at me, the grin on his furry, drool-flecked face as big and stupid-looking as ever.

"Thanks to Kitty," I tell my friends, "we've got ourselves a little more time to try to save the planet."

33.

I TAKE A SEAT ON THE CURB.

I need a second.

A chance for my brain to catch up.

To process the fact that I've now, in the space of a single day, met and spoken with not one, not two, but *three* extraterrestrials—and also, maybe even more mind-bendingly, seen just what one of their terrifying little zap-cannons can do.

"Are you—" Dan starts to ask.

But he's interrupted by a

Beep-beep BOOP.

Dan digs Bem's communication device out of his pocket. I guess he stuck it in there before we all rushed out of my house.

Swiping the screen, angling his head so he can get a better look at the message through all the cracks, Dan reads: "'Tonight on *The Bean Show*, an interview with global superstar Rooparoopamcsewerswapper." Dan gives the screen a few more swipes to make sure that's it, then shoves the thing back into his pocket. "Spam," he says.

I take a deep breath, then quickly catch the others up on what went down with Kermin and Muckle.

"Okay," says Mikaela, after I finish the part where Kermin told me it was conceivable that I wasn't as stupid and useless as I seemed to be. "So there'll be no more zap-cannoning for the rest of the day because of this *dog meeting* the aliens think is happening. We've delayed them, but they're still planning on zapping the rest of the planet to microscopic smithereens and putting up their billboard *tomorrow*."

Dan offers me a hand and pulls me up onto my feet. Together, we all start back to my house.

"So . . . ," Mikaela says. "What are we gonna do?"

I can only think of two options. One: get down on our knees and beg the aliens to pretty, pretty please let us go on existing. Or two: stand up to them, try to put up a fight against their zap-cannons. Unfortunately, both seem incredibly unlikcly to work, so I don't even bother sharing them with the others.

Judging by the thick, knotty silence between us, I know none of them have come up with any brilliant ideas either. At least not by the time we turn the corner onto my street.

And it's there that my feet freeze and my brain completely short-circuits.

Because we can see my house.

And see that Edsley is waiting for us on my lawn.

And see, too, that he's not alone.

Standing beside him is a robot. A robot who appears to have recently participated in the world's most epic food fight.

And just in case there's any confusion about who it is, he calls out to us:

"*Greee*-tings, NIN-com-*poops*."

34.

IT'S *KLAUS*.

The robot, let me remind you, that Edsley built several days ago, after we explicitly told him *not* to build it.

The robot, let me remind you, that Edsley upset to such an extent that he *attacked* the kid and then stormed out of his house.

The robot, let me remind you, that we then spent several unimaginably stressful days searching everywhere for.

The robot, let me remind you, who on multiple occasions nearly ended our lives with his fatally speedy farts.

The robot, let me remind you, who we only *just finally managed* to subdue and, by removing his limbs and head from his torso, render harmless.

And now, it appears, Edsley has gone *AND PUT THE FLIPPING THING BACK TOGETHER AGAIN*.

More or less.

Because I've got one of the bot's arms and legs, plus

a handful of his hard-
ware, up in my bedroom.

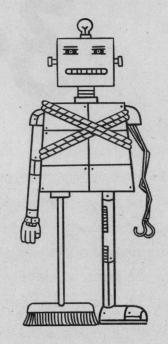

But Edsley used a
duct-tape-reinforced
broomstick in place
of the bot's leg, a few
braided clothes hangers
for an arm, and a couple
of ropes to hold the
guy's torso together.

It's these little details
that finally force my
brain to reboot. And
since it doesn't look
like Klaus is in much of a butt-blasting mood at the
moment, I stomp down the rest of the street and up
onto my lawn.

"*MIKE!*" I shout on my way. "*WHAT—WHAT THE—
WHAT THE—*"

Kitty bolts up from behind me a beat after I make it
onto the grass.

"*RARF! RARF! RARF!*" he roars, running laps around
the robot.

Klaus does his best to keep his eyes on the dog. "The

CAY-nine is up-SETT-ing MY *eee*-QUA-lib-ri-*ummm*," he complains.

A second later, Dan and Mikaela and John Henry Knox are there beside me.

But before they can say anything—or, you know, just angrily gesticulate and shout, like me—Edsley lifts his hands and pushes them toward us in a calming motion.

"Chill," he says.

Which, it seems to me, is basically like telling someone who's just caught fire to relax.

Edsley puffs out his chest, all proud of himself, and says, "I fully reprogrammed Klaus. He's as obedient as a dog."

Just then, Klaus says:

"STOP, CAY-nine. SIT. SIT. SIT."

Kitty, of course, just keeps on barking and circling him.

Edsley deflates a bit.

"Well . . . ," he says. "He's obedient as, like, a *really* obedient dog."

35.

IT'S BEEN MORE THAN A MINUTE SINCE WE

found Edsley and Klaus, and the bot still hasn't fired off a single fart or tried to claw off any of our faces. So, for the time being, I decide to entertain the possibility that in rebuilding and reprogramming the guy, Edsley hasn't made a colossally stupid mistake. Maybe just, you know, a regular-size stupid mistake.

"I don't know what you're up to, Mike," I say, "but we don't have time for it."

"Gimme five minutes," he says.

"No."

"Two."

"*No.*"

"One?"

I glance up at the sky. Because, sure, Kermin and Muckle really seemed to believe me—or, I guess, believe *Kitty*—but what if they've reconsidered, decided to come right back down and recommence their systematic decimation of our planet?

Not seeing any UFO-shaped cumulonimbus clouds sinking out of the sky, I look back down at Mike.

I sigh.

"Fine," I tell him. "Sixty seconds. Show us what he can do so we can get this over with."

Edsley grins. This, it's clear, is what he came over to do. To show off, brag, preen like a peacock.

I head over to my porch, crouch down near the steps, and reach beneath the bottom one. After feeling around for a second, I find one of the emergency rocks I keep stashed there.

"Kitty!" I call, waving the thing around over my head.

Kitty stops barking and circling the bot.

I toss the rock on the lawn, and the pooch darts for it, giving Edsley and Klaus plenty of room to do whatever they're going to do.

"All right, Klaus," Mike says. "Let's show 'em what you've got."

36.

IT'S LIKE WE'RE AT A SCIENCE FAIR, AND WE'RE

the judges and Edsley's presenting. He throws questions and commands at Klaus, starting off nice and simple, but getting increasingly complex.

"What's your name, bot?" he says.

Klaus replies:

"MY *naaame* is KLAUS. HOW-ev-*errr*, I have ALL-so been PRO-*graaamed* to RE-spond to 'DUDE,' '*brooo*,' '*bruuuh*,' 'BUD,' and '*tuuurd* GOB-lin.'"

"Really, Mike?" Mikaela says.

"That doesn't seem necessary," adds John Henry Knox.

Edsley ignores them and goes on.

"Klaus," he says. "What's the longest word in the English language?"

"The LONG-est *wooord* in the EN-glish LANG-uage is PNEUM-o-NOUL-*traaa*-mic-ro-SCOP-ic-SIL-ic-o-VOL-cane-*ooo*-CO-nee-os-IS. The *wooord* CON-tains FOUR-*teee*-FIVE let-*terrrs*."

"Klaus," Edsley says, "perform the following calculation: 24.978 plus 7,082 times 39 divided by 3.14159265359."

"The AN-*sweeer* is EIGHT sev-EN NINE FOUR one *poooint* FIVE *threee* one NINE FOUR FOUR one EIGHT FOUR EIGHT *twooo* NINE sev-EN *threee* SIX."

"Klaus," says Mike, "say, 'Excuse me, Mister. It appears your butt has fallen off. Would you like a grape-fruit?'"

"EX-*cuuuse* ME, Mis-TER. It APP-ears your *buuutt* has FALL-en OFF. Would YOU like a GRAPE-*fruuuit?*"

"Now say, 'Dang it. I have a terrible itch in my kneepit.'"

"*Daaang* IT. I HAVE a terr-IB-ull ITCH in my *kneee-*PIT."

"Now say—"

"Okay, okay, Mike," I say, before he can make the bot say anything else. "We really don't have time for show-and-tell. If you want to stick around and *help* us try to *save the planet,* you're welcome to."

"Wait," says Edsley. He turns to Dan, and all of a sudden he seems nervous. Shy. "What do *you* think, man?"

He probably wants Dan's opinion since Dan's the

one who designed and built and first programmed the bots.

And after a second of thinking about it, Dan says, "Good work, Mike. I'm impressed."

Edsley beams.

And I use the same line on him that Kermin, the alien, used on me:

"It is conceivable," I say, "that you are not as stupid and useless as you seem to be, human. Now can we please get back to—"

And that's when it hits me.

Hits me as hard as the asteroid that wiped out the dinosaurs hit the Yucatán Peninsula down in Mexico sixty-six million years ago.

I think I've got it.

I think I've figured it out.

I think I know what we can do to try to keep the Plerpians from wiping *us* out.

37.

"OH MY GOD. OH MY GOD. OH MY GOD. OH MY
God, oh my God."

"Ken?" says Dan, hurrying over to my side.

"Is he having a heart attack?" asks John Henry Knox.
"It appears he's having a heart attack."

Edsley, being Edsley, assumes that my flipping out is
all about his feat of robotic reprogramming.

"Hold up, Ken," he says. "I know it's crazy amazing,
but you can't die yet. I haven't even shown you the
coolest thing I programmed Klaus to do."

"He's *not* having a heart attack," Mikaela assures
everyone.

She comes closer to me, her eyes narrowed and
trained on mine the entire time.

"You've realized something, haven't you?" she says.
"You've got an idea. About how we can save the planet."

I run it through my head again, just to make sure.

Then, confidently, I nod.

38.

WE DECIDE TO HEAD INSIDE, SINCE THE REST

of my neighborhood's going to start waking up any second and us standing around on my lawn with a walking, talking—but thankfully *not* farting—robot is a really great way to attract attention.

Which, at the moment, we don't want.

We've got work to do.

A whole lot of it.

"Bot," Edsley tells Klaus, "we're gonna go hang out in this nincompoop's house for a bit. Why don't you go and, uh . . ." He scans the area. "How about you go hide behind that tree?"

The bot doesn't hesitate. He spins around and hobbles off in the direction Edsley's pointing. And once he reaches the designated tree, he crouches down and contorts his limbs (including those that are actually clothes hangers and a broomstick) in a way that makes him *almost* completely concealed behind the tree's trunk.

For a second, I wonder whether we should bring the bot into my house and stash him somewhere safer.

But I'm way too eager to share with the others what's whirling around in my mind.

So I grab hold of Kitty, who grabs hold of the rock I gave him, and drag him toward the house.

"Come on," I tell my friends. "We've got a planet to save."

39.

INSIDE, WE FIND DAD IN THE KITCHEN.

Fortunately, he's put on some more clothes since we last saw him.

Unfortunately, he decides to be decidedly *awkward* about the whole underwear incident.

"Oh, um, hey, kids," he says. "Didn't expect you to be back so soon. Though, ah, as you can see"—he shuffles his feet, like he's getting ready to do some kind of dance—"I've got on pants. Because, I mean, I usually do. I didn't expect you all to be here earlier, so that's why I, you know, *didn't*. But whenever I know we'll be having company over, that's one of the first things I do. I say, 'Make sure you have your pants on, Kal. No one wants to see you in your boxer shorts.' Though when you think about it, boxer shorts are basically just like swim trunks. So—"

Mikaela clears her throat, interrupting my dad and, therefore, doing him a HUGE favor.

"Um, Ken's dad?" she says. "Maybe you should just, like, stop talking now."

"Know what?" he tells her. "That's a *fantastic* idea."

He raises his cup of coffee to thank Mikaela, then heads for the living room.

"I'll be in here if you need me!" he calls back.

I turn to Mikaela.

"Thanks," I tell her.

"No prob," she says.

We take seats around the table.

But seconds after we do:

Beep-beep BOOP.

Dan pulls out Bem's communication device.

"Whoa," Edsley says. "What's *that* thing?"

Dan ignores him for the moment and says, "This one's really from Bem." He reads: "'Demo moved up, but then delayed. Tomorrow at noon. After a dog meeting?'"

Edsley's waving his hands, trying to get us to slow down.

"Bem?" he says. "Dog meeting?"

The minutes are ticking by, but we *do* need to catch Mike up on what's going on, otherwise he *really* won't be able to help us.

Dan goes first, giving Edsley a quick rundown of all he learned during his ride on the spaceship.

And Edsley's reaction to all that information?

"Dang. I gotta try some of these *beans*. They must be, like, *SOOO* good."

I go next, telling Mike all about Kermin and Muckle, their zap-cannons, and how I used their unexpected reverence toward dogs in order to buy us a bit more time to figure out how to save the planet.

Edsley says:

"What was the aliens' underwear like? Like ours? Or, like, super advanced?"

"Mike," I say. "I didn't really have a chance to thoroughly investigate the aliens' underwear. And even if I *did*, I don't think I would've taken it."

"Dude. The underwear industry's been due for a revolution for *years* now. If those aliens have something crazy going on, we should totally copy whatever they're doing and take over the undies game."

"Okay," I say, just to shut him up. "We'll do that. Right after we *save the world*."

"Speaking of which . . . ," says Dan.

And then all my friends are staring at me, ready to see if I've actually come up with an idea that can get us out of this mess.

Not to mention our entire planet.

And the rest of the 7.6 billion people living on it.

And the millions of animal species.

And the hundreds of thousands of plant species.

"So?" says John Henry Knox, fiddling with the cover of the *Plerpian Protocols of Planetary Demolition*.

Mikaela says, "Lay it on us."

I take a deep breath.

"Okay. What we have to do," I say, "is convince the Plerpians—especially those who want to turn our planet into a ginormongous billboard—that it's conceivable that humanity is not as stupid and useless as it seems to be."

40.

DON'T WORRY.

There's a bit more to my plan than that.

"The Plerpians think we're a bunch of idiots," I say. "Selfish, destructive, careless idiots."

"They're wrong, though," Mikaela says.

"Exactly!" I cry.

"I mean," she goes on, "the only thing I've ever really *destroyed* is my mom's computer, back when I was nine years old. But then I rebuilt it and made it twenty times faster and sixty-seven times more powerful, so."

I say it again:

"Exactly!"

Then Dan sweeps a hand around the table, indicating all of us.

"And *we* care about the planet. And I *know* we can't be the only ones out there who do."

I say it one more time:

"Exactly!"

"And we are *certainly* not idiots," adds John Henry Knox.

I hesitate before saying *exactly* again, my eyes sliding over to Edsley. True to form, he says:

"Yeah. Would a bunch of idiots be thinking about how to revolutionize the underwear industry? I think *not.*"

To that, I'm really not sure what to say.

So I just ignore it.

As do Dan, Mikaela, and John Henry Knox.

After which they all start nodding.

And smiling.

And seeing this, I'm feeling good.

No.

I'm feeling *great.*

Full of energy.

Full of confidence.

Full of that feeling that lets me know that I, with the help of my friends, can accomplish literally *ANYTHING.*

It's the feeling I get whenever the EngiNerds tackle a problem together.

Like we could gather up a bunch of our parents'

vacuum cleaners and build a hovercraft—which, yeah, is something we actually did.

Or hole ourselves up in my basement for a weekend and construct an automated, two-in-one, snowball/sno-*cone* maker—again, something we actually did (in addition to finding out just how many sno-cones you have to eat in a single afternoon before you never want to see one of the things again).

Or even, you know, save our planet from being turned into a bunch of dust and replaced by a *bean* billboard.

I'm so pumped up, I can't even sit down any longer.

I leap to my feet.

I slam the butt of my fist down on the table.

"Let's *do* this!" I cry.

"YES," says Dan.

And just from his eyes, I can tell he's full of the same nerdy, we-can-accomplish-literally-anything energy that I am.

As is Mikaela.

And John Henry Knox.

(And Edsley, even if some of *his* energy is busy thinking about underwear.)

And they're just looking at me.

And looking at me.

 122

And looking at me some more.

Finally, John Henry Knox tosses the *Plerpian Protocols of Planetary Demolition* onto the table and blurts out:

"SO HOW ARE WE GONNA DO IT?!"

I gulp.

Then sit back down in my chair.

Quietly, I admit:

"I, uh, haven't gotten that far yet."

41.

I TRY TO KEEP THAT NERDY, WE-CAN-

accomplish-literally-anything energy alive.

But I can feel it draining from my friends, a little more every second.

We need to figure something out—a next step, at the very least, if not enough steps to make up a whole plan—otherwise the same thing's going to happen as happened last week when I was trying to get all the rest of the EngiNerds to keep helping me look for Klaus. When you bang your head up against a problem long enough, you can get discouraged, and then dispirited, and then desperate to just switch gears and do something even a tiny bit easier. But what we're facing here—this is the *ultimate* problem. We can't afford to lose focus. We can't afford to fail.

"Maybe . . . ," I try.

"What if we . . . ," says Dan.

"We could . . . ," Mikaela says, scratching her head.

"How about . . . ," adds John Henry Knox.

And then Edsley chimes in with, "I'm pretty sure they call farts *parps*."

I look over and see that he's reading from the *Plerpian Protocols of Planetary Demolition*.

Before I can remind him that I said he could stay at my house only if he actually *helped* us, my dad shouts to us from the living room.

"Ken! Get in here! You've gotta see what's on the news!"

I don't answer. Because I'm not interested in the news right now. Because, if we don't solve this problem of ours soon, there are going to be a couple of aliens zap-cannoning their way through town on the news.

But Dad doesn't quit.

"Seriously, Ken! Hurry up! Remember those robots last week? There's another one!"

That gets our attention.

A beat later, we're all on our feet and rushing to get a look at the TV.

42.

WE MAKE IT TO THE LIVING ROOM JUST IN

time to hear John Castle, field reporter for the Channel 5 News Team, whisper, "Is this robot somehow related to those that recently menaced our town with their furiously fast farts?"

John is whispering because he's crouched behind a bush, clearly quite traumatized from his previous encounter with the flatulent machines.

The camera pans to show the robot—it's Klaus, of course. I can tell right away thanks to the broomstick leg and ropes circling his torso. But the bot doesn't appear to be doing anything *too* menacing at the moment. He's hobbling up the street, pausing every few feet and angling his body so that he can reach down to the pavement. Using the arm that hasn't been replaced by a bunch of twisted clothes hangers, he plucks up what looks like an old, dirty napkin. He carries the thing over to the curb, and thanks to a well-timed zoom-in from the camera, we can see the bot place the grimy square of paper atop a small pile of leaves, twigs, and other bits of litter.

The camera pulls out and refocuses on John Castle.

"It would seem," the reporter says, ditching his whisper now that Klaus has put some more distance between them, "that the robot is engaged in some sort of pre-fart ritual. The Channel 5 News Team is committed to monitoring this situation in the event that—"

The camera spins and twists as if whoever's holding the thing just randomly decided to do a backflip.

A beat later, there's a shriek.

And the next thing the camera shows is John Castle dashing down the street as fast as his fancy dress shoes allow, the cord of his microphone trailing behind him like a long, twitchy snake.

My stomach drops.

"Um, Dad?" I say. "We're gonna head out again. Something just came up."

I take a step toward the kitchen.

But none of my friends follow me.

Their eyes are glued to the chaotic scene unfolding on the screen.

I give each of their shirts a tug to snag their attention, then herd them into the kitchen and toward the door.

"Be careful!" my dad calls after us. "Don't get, ah, farted at!"

43.

OUTSIDE, I HURRY TOWARD THE TREE THAT

Klaus had been tucked behind just a few minutes ago. Scanning the ground right around it, I find a handful of small depressions—little craters the same size and shape as the butt end of a broomstick. I follow a path of these evenly spaced indentations across my lawn, all the way to the curb. Then: nothing. Obviously. Even if Klaus weighed a thousand pounds, his broomstick leg couldn't put a divot in the pavement of the street.

"THERE!"

It's Mikaela, darting a little ways up the street and then pointing down at the curb.

The rest of us rush over and take a look.

And there, perched on the rounded stretch of pavement, is a small pile of leaves and rocks and gum wrappers.

"Another one!" Mikaela shouts, pointing a little ways farther up the street, to where there's a second small pile of debris sitting atop the curb.

I spin around and peer down the street in the other direction. And it takes only a couple seconds for me to pick out a bunch of rocks, a sun-bleached bottle wrapper, and some crunched-up leaves scattered about the pavement.

And while I've got no clue just what in the world Klaus is up to, it's pretty clear how we can find him.

44.

WE FIND KLAUS JUST A FEW BLOCKS AWAY.

John Castle and his cameraperson are nowhere in sight. I'm not sure what spooked them, but I guess they gave up on monitoring the situation for Channel 5 News watchers.

The bot hears us behind him and pauses in his street cleaning to turn his head and greet us.

"*Greee*-tings, NIN-com-*poops*."

He doesn't wait for us to respond. Just turns around and goes back to de-littering the patch of pavement he'd been working on before we arrived.

I lean over, hands to knees, and catch my breath. I've probably done more running today than I have in the past couple years combined.

Mikaela recovers quicker than I do, so she asks Edsley the question all of us are no doubt wondering.

"What is he *doing*?"

"Cleaning my room," Edsley answers. "Or, I mean, that's what he *thinks* he's doing. You really think I'd just reprogram the bot to be an overgrown calculator and repeat whatever stupid sentences I wanted him to?" He chuckles. "Of course not. I reprogrammed him to be an overgrown calculator, repeat whatever stupid sentences I want him to, *and* do all my chores."

Mikaela takes a step closer to the bot. She narrows her eyes. I can tell her thoughts are zipping and zooming about in her brain. I don't know what it is, but she's on the verge of figuring *something* out.

"Keep talking, Mike . . . ," she says.

"Um, sure," he says. "Okay. Yeah. Talk, talk, talk. I'm talking. I'm talking. I'm still talking." He turns it into a song. *"I'm talking 'cause Mikaela loves the sound of my voice, 'cause it sounds so—"*

I give Edsley a shove.

"Keep talking about the *bot*," I tell him.

"Oh," Mike says. "Uhh, well, he can feed my cat and also scoop the poop out of my cat's litter box and dump it in the trash. And then, once it's full, he can take out the trash, and then even put a new bag in the trash can, which I *hate* doing, because the stupid thing was clearly designed by a turd goblin of the highest order and it always pinches my fingers. And he—the bot, not the turd goblin of a trash can designer—was supposed to clean just *my* room, but I think I messed up that part of the programming a little, so I guess he kind of thinks the whole planet is my room." He shrugs. "Dan's design is so good that, as long as you know what you're doing, you can get one of these bad boys to do pretty much anything at all."

Mikaela's eyes are no longer narrow.

They're wide open.

Unblinking and ticking back and forth like she's chasing down one particular thought ricocheting around her brain.

I'm watching her, trying to catch up with her thinking, since I've obviously failed to *keep* up.

Abruptly, her eyes stop.

A grin slips onto her lips.

"Klaus?" she says.

The bot stiffens.

Stands up straight.

Turns to face her.

"NIN-com-*poop*?"

"We've got a different kind of mess for you to clean up," Mikaela says.

Beside me, Dan—who must have more of a clue than I do what Mikaela's thinking—takes a shaky breath.

"A *mess*?" asks Klaus.

Mikaela nods.

"A really, really big one."

45.

"THE *WAAAY* YOU ARE LOOK-ING AT *MEEE*
has *meee* mod-ERR-utt-*lee* CON-cerned," Klaus tells
Mikaela.

"Don't worry," she says. "You're about to take the
trip of a lifetime."

"Wait a second," says Edsley. "Why are we sending
Klaus to Disneyland? And can I go with him?"

"*Mike*," I say. "Mikaela's not saying we should send
the bot to *Disneyland*." I lean toward Mikaela and, quietly, add, "You're not, right?"

"Of course not," John Henry Knox answers for her.
"Mikaela's proposing we send Klaus to Plerp-5. She's
suggesting that Dan's creation could, perhaps, convince the planet's Planetary Leadership that humans
aren't *all* selfish, careless, destructive idiots."

"Oh," Edsley says.

And then, a second later:

"*Ooohhhh.*"

And then, *another* second later:

"Well, can I go with him *there*?"

"Definitely *not*," I say, freshly aware of just how much trouble Edsley's capable of causing on his own planet, and not the least bit interested in learning what he can do on someone else's.

"Think about it," Mikaela says, eyeing Klaus again. "The bot constitutes an impressive feat of design work, construction abilities, *and* programming skills. If that doesn't show the Plerpians that we're not all fools, I don't know what will. Also, Dan built the bots to respond to a problem, right? Because he *cares*. Not just about himself, but about humanity as a whole. I mean, I know it's not a *perfect* plan. I know it's not a slam dunk. But we don't have a lot of time here. If we sit around hoping for an idea like that? It'll be morning before we know it."

We're all silent, thinking things through.

Finally, Edsley says, "It *is* a pretty solid idea. It's just too bad I kinda manhandled Klaus's insides when I reprogrammed him."

Dan looks concerned.

"What do you mean, 'manhandled'?"

Edsley aims a finger at Klaus.

"Let's just say that that guy's insides look more like a bowl of spaghetti than a motherboard."

"Oh-*kay*," Mikaela says. "So can't we just go in there, clean up the wiring, and—"

"Noooooo," Edsley interrupts. "No, no, no, no, no. You don't want to open him back up. That rope there's the only thing holding his torso together. And the front panel—that's holding the toilet paper roll in place. And if the toilet paper roll gets knocked out of place, then the toothbrush could hit the wiring and—"

SPZZT!

A spark arcs out of Klaus's neck.

I leap back, just in time to see the little, white-hot flame land on the pavement where one of my feet had just been. It fizzles out in a fraction of a second, leaving a small black smear on the street.

SPZZZZT!

SPZZT-SPZZT-SPZZT!

SPZZzZZzzZzZzzzzZZZzZZzZZZZZZZZT!

"Uh-oh," Edsley says, the sparks now coming out of Klaus's neck fast and furious, obscuring the bot's head and creating an on-the-spot, several-weeks-early Independence Day fireworks show. Except, you know, *way* more dangerous.

Within seconds, the air is busy with noise and smoke.

My lungs begin to burn.

I can't see a thing.

But just as suddenly as the sparks started, they stop.

I peer into the thick cloud of smoke, hoping what I never could've imagined I would—that Klaus is okay.

46.

WHEN THE SMOKE FINALLY CLEARS, KLAUS'S
head—it's *gone*.

It's just . . . no longer there.

Not atop the robot's head.

Not on the ground.

Not anywhere.

It's like the thing got nailed by a Plerpian zap-cannon.

But the bot's still standing.

Briefly.

Then, with one last *SPZZT!* and a handful of sparks, he tips forward and—*CLANK!*—slams down onto the pavement.

47.

"MICHAEL!!!"

That'd be me, shouting at Edsley.

And Edsley, calmly as a refrigerated cucumber, says, "Yeah?"

"Do you REALIZE," I ask him, "that you MIGHT'VE. JUST. DESTROYED. OUR LAST. CHANCE. TO SAVE. THE PLANET?!?!?!"

Edsley doesn't have any real reaction.

He doesn't look the least bit remorseful.

Not even slightly worried.

"Can't we just use the other robot?" he asks.

"WHAT other robot?" I demand.

"The last one Dan made. The one that was never built. The one that you've got some of, and Dan's got some of, and Jerry's got some of, and John Henry Knox's got some of."

The eighteenth bot, I think as I picture the duct-taped box of parts stashed under my bed.

"Oh," I say. "Yeah. I—I guess we could do that."

48.

WE GATHER UP WHAT REMAINS OF KLAUS

and haul him back to my house as quickly as we can.

I check the sky again, making sure there are still no cumulonimbus clouds sinking down out of it.

"So are we doing this?" Dan calls out loud enough to be heard over our street-slapping sneakers. "Will it really work?"

"Now's not the time to be humble," I call back to him.

"I'm not," says Dan. "But the bots—they didn't exactly run smoothly."

"So they had some minor flaws," I say.

"Minor?!" cries Dan.

"In the grand scheme of things," I argue. "I mean—"

"KEN," Edsley interjects. "I'm pretty sure Dan means the farting! The super-fast farting the robots did!"

"I know!" I say. "But with all of us—"

"And maybe also the punching!" Edsley adds. "He might also mean the punching and the kicking and the stomping and the clawing."

"With all of us working together—"

"And the head-butting! Didn't one of them head-butt someone too?"

"I *think* what Kennedy might be trying to say," says John Henry Knox, "is that, with all of us working together, we may be able to reprogram the last bot in a completely flaw-free way."

"Aha!" Edsley says.

I just shake my head and adjust my grip on the robot parts I'm carrying.

"But," says Mikaela, "before we do that, we have to decide what to program the bot to do. It's got to be really—"

"TEAMWORK MAKES THE DREAM WORK!"

It's Edsley, charging out ahead of us, hoisting a hunk of Klaus's torso up over his head like it's some kind of trophy.

"He's not wrong!" Dan calls out to us.

"Come on, then," says Mikaela, picking up her pace to keep up with Edsley. "LET'S DO THIS!"

49.

WHEN WE'RE STILL ABOUT A BLOCK AWAY

from my house, Dan calls out, "Ken!"

I turn to him in time to see him toss me the robot leg that he's been holding.

Snatching it out of the air, I ask him, "Going home to get your share of the bot parts?"

He nods, then veers off in another direction.

John Henry Knox says, "I will too!"

Then he chucks the robot arm that *he's* been holding toward Edsley. But the throw isn't exactly a great one—in fact, it's downright tragic—and even though Mike makes a valiant attempt to catch the thing, it just ends up smacking him in the side of the head.

"My bad!" cries John Henry Knox as he hurries down a side street.

I slow my stride and angle my steps so I can scoop up the arm, then call out to Edsley, "You all right?"

"NO PAIN, NO GAIN!" he shouts back.

Which doesn't *really* apply to this situation.

But I suppose I appreciate the sentiment behind it.

With Edsley a few strides in front of us, Mikaela and I follow him the rest of the way to my house. There, I dump what I've got of Klaus on the lawn and lead the way up the front steps, across the porch, and inside.

Right away I grab the phone and dial Jerry's number.

Because if we're really going to get this job done, we're going to need as many EngiNerds as we can get.

50.

THE THREE RINGS IT TAKES FOR SOMEONE

to answer the phone at Jerry's house feel like three *eternities.*

But luckily, it's Jerry who finally does answer.

"Hello?" he says normally enough.

And I say something along the lines of:

"*Jerrythere'snotimetosayhellorightnowthisisridiculouslyimportantandtimeisoftheessencedoyourememberhowweneverbuiltyourrobotandwesplititupintofourpilesofpartsandIkeptoneandsodidDanandJohnHenryKnoxandyouwellwethinkthebotmightbetheanswertosavingthewholeworldohyeahIforgottofillyouinonhowthesealienscalledPlerpiansaregonnablowupourplanetsotheycanputupaginormongousbillboardfortheirbeansbutbacktotherobotpartscanyoupleasedropeverythingyouaredoingandbringthemovertomyhouserightnow?*"

At first, Jerry says nothing.

And then—pretty reasonably, I suppose—he says, "Uhhh . . ."

Mikaela grabs the phone from me.

"Jerry?" she says. "It's Mikaela. If we can convince the aliens that human beings aren't *all* selfish, stupid, destructive idiots, we're pretty sure we can save the planet from being permanently terminated. To do that, we're gonna need you to bring over those robot parts you've got under your bed."

I can't hear what Jerry says, but it must be affirmative.

Because half a second later, Mikaela says, "See you soon," and hangs up the phone.

And that's when a voice that isn't mine or hers or Edsley's enters the conversation.

"Is everything all right in here, kids?"

We all whirl around and see my dad, standing there in the doorway with his coffee cup in one hand and an empty bowl of cereal in the other. Based on his question and the mostly confused, partly panicked look on his face, I can only assume he's been standing there since we barreled into the house, too caught up in saving the planet to notice that we weren't alone.

Mikaela looks at me.

I look at her.

But before either one of us can figure out how to

respond, Edsley answers my dad—and answers *honestly*.

"Not really," he says. "But give us a few hours, and it will be."

"Probably," Mikaela hedges.

"*Hope*fully," I say.

Dad says, "Oh-*kay* . . ." Then he gestures across the kitchen with his cereal bowl. "Can I just get to the sink?"

We step aside.

My dad crosses the room and drops his dishes in the sink. Then, giving us one last confused glance, he returns to the living room to sit on the couch and continue having a regular old run-of-the-mill day.

51.

THANKS TO HIS SKILLS ON HIS SKATEBOARD,

Jerry gets to my house before either Dan or John Henry Knox.

Mikaela, Edsley, and I meet him out on my lawn.

Right away, Jerry and I get to work opening our boxes of robot parts and laying them out on the grass.

While we're at it, Mikaela fills Jerry in on the rest of what he's missed.

Edsley jumps in here and there, making sure Jerry gets all the *most* important details. Like how the Plerpian demolition crew were dressed as normal adult humans—minus *pants*. Or how since, because *he* was the one who proved that the bots could be more or less flawlessly reprogrammed, he's sort of responsible for saving the planet.

"Let's not get ahead of ourselves," I tell Mike. "We haven't even figured out what we're going to reprogram the bot to do."

A surge of nervousness runs through my body.

Because even though I really do believe that the EngiNerds, working together, can do anything—*including* save the planet—that doesn't mean it's going to be easy.

Most likely, it's going to be very, *very* far from it.

52.

DAN AND JOHN HENRY KNOX SHOW UP JUST

a couple minutes after Jerry and I've finished organizing our robot parts on the lawn. And just a couple minutes after *that*, we've got their parts added to the bunch.

We step back and look at it all.

"Okay," says Dan. "First, we've got to figure out what we want the bot to do. Then we can work backward and see if we can tinker with the design and program it to actually *do* it."

"So, what do we want it to do?" I say. "What sort of function would most impress these Plerpians? What would blow them away to the point where they'd say, 'We can't zap this awesome species and their wonderful-if-damaged planet into a whole bunch of nothingness. We've got to keep them around'?"

"Oh! Oh!"

It's Edsley.

I prepare myself for the worst—while also, perhaps stupidly, hoping for the best.

"These aliens love beans, right?" Edsley says.

"Right . . . ," says Dan, a hint of hesitation in his voice.

"But *maybe*," Edsley continues, a big grin sliding onto his face, "they don't all love to *cook*."

I sigh.

"We're not going to program the bot to cook beans, Mike," I say.

He's still grinning.

"Duh," he says. "We're gonna program it to cook, bake, roast, sear, stir-fry, *and* sauté beans."

"You can sauté beans?" says Jerry.

Mikaela clears her throat.

"Let's keep it on the list of options, Mike," she says. "But we should probably come up with some others. Just to make sure we're choosing the absolute best."

We all go back to thinking.

"Part of what made Dan's creation so incredible," John Henry Knox says after a minute, "is that it addressed a problem."

"Well," says Dan, never one to shut up and just accept a compliment, "a *hypothetical* problem."

"Sure," admits John Henry Knox. "When Dan

designed, built, and programmed the bots, we didn't actually *need* them to venture out into inhospitable environments to gather food for us. But the bots were inspired, at least initially, by my weather-related theorizing and my predictions of an admittedly-distant-but-not-so-distant-that-we-shouldn't-be-preparing-for-it future in which we *did* need them for that. He was anticipating a problem. Attempting to solve it before it even truly *became* a problem. Some might argue that that is even *more* brilliant than solving a problem that's staring you right in the face."

"But we're leaving the *people* out of the equation," Mikaela says. "The people and, in this case, the *aliens*. Because they're doing the same thing, aren't they? They think *they're* going to solve a bunch of problems by zapping our planet into a bunch of piles of dust and replacing it with a billboard. Because we know humans have been causing damage to *our* planet, but now it looks like we might be causing harm to the rest of our solar system, and soon maybe even the whole entire *galaxy*. We've got to show the Plerpians that we've got what it takes to address *that*. That we can make a contribution to the galaxy. That we can actually be really great neighbors. Ones that it might benefit *them* to keep around."

"You're right," says Edsley. "Which is why," he adds, "whatever we reprogram the bot to do, I don't think it could hurt to *also* have the guy know how to cook a can of beans."

53.

IT TAKES HOURS FOR US TO SETTLE ON
exactly what we're going to attempt to reprogram the
robot to do.

That might sound crazy.

But the decision isn't an easy one.

It's probably the most important decision we'll make
in our entire lives.

We have to do something impressive.

Something big and bold.

But we're on a *seriously tight* schedule, which of
course limits just how ambitious we can be.

The whole time we're debating and arguing and,
at one point, kinda sorta *fighting* with one another, I
can hear a clock ticking in my head. The sky is still
cloudy—though cumulonimbus-free—but I can sense
the sun dipping lower and lower. Noon tomorrow really
isn't all that far away.

In the end, none of us are exactly thrilled with what
we land on. I feel a lot like I did the time I totally spaced

on a science project and had to put the thing together in a single evening. I still got an A-minus—not to brag or anything—but it bothered me, because I knew that if I'd been working on the project all month long, I could've done something absolutely EPIC.

"So," I say, once our conversation quiets. "We're in agreement."

"*If*," Edsley stipulates, "we can include that thing I talked about."

Dan reaches for Bem's communication device.

"Now," he says, "let's see what Bem thinks."

"Can you really send him a message on that?" I ask.

"I think so," says Dan. "It's kind of confusing, but I—"

Mikaela clears her throat.

I look, and see that she's holding her hand out to Dan.

Dan sets the communication device in her palm.

Mikaela's thumbs get to work right away, moving over the screen at lightning speed. Within a few seconds, she tells us, "Ready."

Dang. She's got *skills*.

"What should we say?" asks Mikaela.

"Um," Dan says. "Tell him we've got a plan."

Mikaela's thumbs get back to tapping.

 155

"And that we want to run it by him before we get to work," Dan continues.

Mikaela nods and, it seems, sends the message.

Half a second later, we hear:

Beep-beep BOOP.

"That was fast," I say.

Mikaela shakes her head, then reads: "'Have you tried the bean that consumers and critics alike are calling "life-altering" and "revolutionary"? Get your Plerp-12 Super Beans wherever the best beans are sold.'"

"Oh," I say.

We wait, all our eyes glued to the device in Mikaela's hands.

"Come on, Bem . . . ," mutters Dan.

Nothing.

Beep-beep BOOP.

Mikaela checks the screen . . . and sighs. Then she reads:

"'Would a floogleflimp driver change flimps mid-race? Of course, not. So why would you stop enjoying beans from the galaxy's oldest, most-trusted bean producer? Plerp-5 Beans—Your Family's Favorite for a Reason.'"

"Here," says Dan, holding a hand out for the device. "Let me see?"

Mikaela hands him the thing, and Dan gives it a shake, like maybe *that* will get Bem to answer.

It doesn't.

"Tick. Tock. Tick. Tock."

It's Edsley, wagging a finger back and forth.

"Perhaps we should begin to pursue our plan while we wait for Bem to return our message," says John Henry Knox.

"It can't hurt," Jerry agrees.

"Our message sent," Mikaela tells Dan. "He'll see it."

Dan gives the communication device one more shake, then shoves it into his pocket and turns his attention to the pieces and parts of the eighteenth and final robot spread out at our feet.

I do the same.

"All right," I tell the others. "Let's get all this inside. We'll set up in my basement. I should have all the tools and supplies we'll need down there."

I reach down to scoop up a pile of robot parts—but Mikaela stops me with a "Hey."

I look up.

She eyes me, then eyes each of the others in turn.

"We can do this," she tells us.

She lifts an eyebrow and says it again—but this time, we all repeat it with her.

"We can do this."

And then we get to work.

54.

MY MOOD IMPROVES AS SOON AS I'VE GOT

some tools in my hands and a job to do. I wouldn't say that it gets quite within the "good" range—the situation is way too dire for *that*. But it's certainly better than the other moods I've been in today, which have all been of the dark, dreary, and desperate variety.

I can tell the rest of the crew is feeling better, too. Sometimes, making a plan and taking the first steps to execute it is the best way to get yourself out of a funk. Even if that plan isn't perfect. And ours definitely is *not*.

But we're doing the best we can.

And when it comes to the EngiNerds? Well, our best is pretty darn good.

Then:

Beep-beep BOOP.

Bem finally gets in touch, and I'm all of a sudden sharply aware that my recently improved mood might be about to take a major nosedive.

"It's him," Dan tells us, his eyes flicking back and

forth across the screen. "He was—oh jeez—he ate another one of those Food-Plus veggie burgers and then had to go to the bathroom and he—oh. Oh, wow. *Ugh*. Did NOT need to know *that*. TMI, Bem."

Edsley hurries over to take a look at the communication device.

Mikaela steps in his way right before he reaches Dan. She grabs the gadget, and her thumbs start flying over the screen. She reads to us as she types, her message a quick overview of our plan.

And just a couple seconds after she hits send:

Beep-beep BOOP.

"He says . . . ," says Mikaela.

My heart hitches in my chest.

"He says that it 'just might work,'" she finishes reading.

"Okay," I say, getting out ahead of my own disappointment, and hoping to do the same for the others. Because that's not exactly the vote of confidence I was looking for. "*Okay*. That's better than him saying it's a *bad* idea," I assure everyone. "That means we're on the right track." Then I end my little impromptu pep talk with the same encouraging phrase Mikaela used earlier: "We can *do* this."

Dan nods and gulps at the same time.

"Ask him if he can meet us once we've got the bot up and running," he tells Mikaela, her thumbs once again twitching and tapping.

I don't need to ask to know what Dan's thinking. He wants to do a test run for the alien. He wants to show Bem what the bot can do, then take whatever feedback he's got and use it to make any last-minute tweaks we can to really up our chances of knocking the socks off Kermin and Muckle. And we'll have time to do all that, as long as we get the bot properly programmed a few hours before noon tomorrow, when the Plerpian demolition crew is set to return to Earth and recommence their work.

Beep-beep BOOP.

"He says he will," Mikaela tells us. "He says he can come back down to Feldman's Field for a bit once we're ready for him. Also that, even if he's up in the air, he can help make sure the demo crew sees the bot before they zap anything else."

Hearing all this, my mood inches a bit closer to the "good" territory. And even though I was pretty upset with Bem just that morning, now I'm feeling grateful for him, and for all he's done for us. Because earlier, in my fear and confusion, I was hoping the alien would just do all the work, that he'd save our planets *for* us. But that was never his job. Earth isn't *his* planet. He went above and beyond to make sure we were fully aware of the danger it was in. But it always has been—and still is—up to *us* to save it.

We get back to work, and we've got the robot just about half-built—and have made sure to deactivate the bit of the design that causes the bots to finish building their half-built selves—when my stomach lets out a crazy loud growl.

Not a second later, Edsley's does the same.

"Yeah, I wasn't gonna say anything . . . ," Mikaela says, setting a hand on her own stomach. "But, same."

I tuck the wrench I'd been using into my pocket, cross my arms, and stare at the limbless bot torso lying on the floor. Then I check the window, through which I can see a small patch of sky. There's still some light left, but it's the soft, end-of-the-day kind. It must be five thirty or six o'clock by now.

We haven't even gotten to the programming part yet. And while I can't know for sure what sort of snags we'll encounter then, I know there'll be some. (There are *always* unforeseen obstacles.)

"This is gonna take all night," says Dan.

I nod.

Then say:

"Slumber party?"

We head upstairs. I make sure my parents are cool with having everyone over, then the others take turns calling their parents and making sure it's cool with them. And speaking of snags, we hit a slight one there: John Henry Knox's little sisters refuse to put his mom on the phone for a whole fifteen minutes, relenting only when the poor kid agrees to their demands and sings "I'm a Little Teapot" six times in a row in a super high-pitched voice.

But otherwise, it's smooth sailing.

My parents even offer to order us some pizza.

To hold us over while we wait for it to arrive, I fix us up an appetizer of popcorn and peanut butter—the very best brain food there is, in *my* humble opinion. I bring it down to the basement along with some waters and we get back to it.

55.

WE WORK.

And work and work and work.

We eat our pizza.

And work.

We polish off a couple pints of ice cream.

And work.

Ten o'clock becomes eleven o'clock becomes midnight becomes one.

And we work.

And work and work and work.

And I know this might sound a little weird . . .

But I have a ridiculous amount of fun.

Like, an absolute *blast*.

And all my friends do too.

Yes, we're still very much aware that we're working to save the planet, and also still very much aware that our attempt to do so might totally *fail*. But I think that's it. It's like back when I looked at that tree and, newly aware of the threat that it and everything else was under, was all of a sudden bowled over by the thing's miraculousness. We can't *ever* know what the future might bring. But at the moment, we're not even sure there's going to *be* a future. And I guess that's forcing me to fully live in each and every one of these long, hard hours, to sap every bit of life out of each minute, every second. And tomorrow morning, if we all get turned into piles of dust . . . well, I'll be glad to know that I spent my final night on the planet programming a robot with my amazing friends. (And yes, that "amazing" even applies to Edsley and John Henry Knox.)

As expected, we hit some snags. We encounter plenty of unforeseen obstacles.

But we adjust.

We adapt.

We push through.

We just. Keep. Going.

Around four in the morning, we finally get the robot up and running.

But the guy's not quite stage-ready yet.

We do a test run, then another, and then another and another and another, each time finding more little bugs that we've got to fix.

Another hour later, and the robot—whose name,

we learn, is Björn—performs his new functions three times in a row without any issues.

Unless you count as an "issue" this thing he does with his voice. It only happens when he says his name. He tends to get stuck—sort of like sometimes happens with my dad's old CDs when he plays them in the car.

Dan once again fiddles with the wiring inside the bot before closing him up and tightening the last of the screws.

"Say your name," he commands the bot.

I cross my fingers.

But the bot says, "I am BjööööööÖÖRrrrrRrRRRRr-rrrnnNNNNNNNNNNNNNNNNNNNNN—"

Edsley nudges Dan aside and smacks the bot on the back.

"—NNNNNN," the bot concludes.

I check the time.

It's 5:49.

I look back at Dan, his eyes big and bloodshot and seriously sleep-deprived. But despite not having gotten a wink of sleep for two nights in a row, he's frowning hard at the bot. And I know what that look means. It means he wants to keep working, to tinker till his fingers ache, to tweak and test and tweak and test Björn until he runs absolutely flawlessly a thousand times in a row.

"We should get to the field," I urge Dan. "We can keep working there. And Bem can help us."

Jerry, Edsley, and John Henry Knox all nod in agreement.

Mikaela grabs the communication device and fires off a message to Bem.

Dan gives the bot one last look. Then he tucks his screwdriver into his belt and says, "All right. Let's go."

56.

WE SET OUT TOWARD FELDMAN'S FIELD. JUST

your average group of six kids and their recently built and reprogrammed robot, on their way to try to keep the planet from being erased from the universe. Above us, the nighttime sky is giving way to dawn, the color of the horizon-crowding clouds growing a hint softer and brighter with each passing minute.

I keep glancing up at them, figuring I'll see a big, spaceship-camouflaging cumulonimbus cloud slip apart from the rest and sink toward the ground.

But we reach the field before that happens.

And there, I find out why.

Because the big, spaceship-camouflaging cumulonimbus cloud is already parked on the field's patchy grass.

A little nervous tremor rolls through my body. Because what if *Bem* isn't even impressed by our bot? What if he says that the thing doesn't stand a chance of convincing the aliens in charge of his planet to not get rid of us and ours?

We're still about fifty feet away from the ship when the cloud's tufts and puffs part to reveal a metal, charcoal-colored door.

And we're probably about thirty-five feet away when the door opens up.

By the time the ramp pokes out and reaches for the ground, we're only about twenty feet away.

We make it just a few more steps before we all stop short. And there, a not-so-little nervous tremor rolls through my body, making me actually, physically shake.

Because it's not Bem who steps out of the spaceship and starts down the ramp.

It's a pair of aliens.

They're both wearing collared button-down shirts and bright striped ties and—you got it—underpants but no *pants* pants.

It's Kermin and Muckle.

The demolition crew.

Back several hours before they're supposed to be.

And it looks like Muckle finally found his zap-cannon. . . .

57.

WATCHING KERMIN AND MUCKLE DESCEND

the ramp of their spaceship and stride out onto the patchy grass of Feldman's Field, I can't help but think about Klaus.

Because it wasn't so long ago that we were standing in this very same spot, dodging the furious farts of that angry, angry robot.

And why was he so angry with us?

Well, let me remind you:

It was because I had *tricked* him, fooled him into thinking something—a WORLD-FAMOUS CAN'T-MISS MUST-ATTEND TOTALLY AWE-SOME EPICALLY EXCELLENT FESTIVAL OF COMESTIBLES—was going to happen when, in fact, it was not.

And that's pretty much what I did to these two pants-less, canine-obsessed aliens. I'd convinced Kermin and Muckle that I could translate for Kitty

then made up a bunch of stuff about a super important *dog meeting*. I can only assume that they finally
realized I was full of it and are now back to make me
pay for it—along with every other living thing on the
planet.

58.

KERMIN AND MUCKLE QUICKLY CLOSE THE
distance between us and them, stopping just a few feet
in front of us.

I do my best to keep my eyes on theirs, but my gaze
keeps flicking down to the zap-cannons in their hands.

"GREETINGS, HUMAN," Kermin shouts at me. "I
UNDERSTAND THAT, DUE TO YOUR VERY LIM-
ITED MENTAL CAPACITY, YOU HAVE NO DOUBT
ALREADY FORGOTTEN, BUT WE HAVE PREVI-
OUSLY MET." The alien sets a hand on his chest. "I
AM KERMINFLAPPER." Pointing to Muckle, he adds,
"THIS IS MY ASSOCIATE, MUCKLEMCDUNK. WE
ARE THOSE WHO WERE SENT TO METHODI-
CALLY DEMOLISH YOUR FASCINATING AND
BEAUTIFUL PLANET."

Kermin pauses here and looks down at my feet.

"HUMAN. YOU HAVE MISPLACED YOUR
CANINE?"

It's impossible to tell from his tone of voice just what he's up to.

Is he testing me?

Toying with me?

Just making me squirm a bit before he zap-cannons me into a pile of Kennedy-colored dust?

"ALSO," Kermin asks, evidently having only now noticed the robot behind me, "WHAT IS THE IDENTITY OF THIS SHINY BEING?"

Before I can answer, Björn steps forward and says, "*Greee*-TINGS. I am BJÖööÖöÖÖöÖöÖRRrrrrRrR-RRRRRrrrrrrrrrrrrrrrrrrrrrrrrrrrrr—"

Edsley delivers a few firm slaps to the bot's back. But it's not shutting him up like it did back on my lawn.

"—*rrrrrrrRrRrrrRRRrrr*RRRRRRRRRRRRRRRRRR-RRRRRRR—"

Edsley slaps again.

And again.

But it only makes things worse.

"—*RrrnNnNnNnnnNNNNNNööööÖRrrrrrrnJBbBb-JbÖÖÖÖÖöö*—"

Dan slides his screwdriver out of his pocket and heads for the bot.

Just as, out of the corner of my eye, I see Muckle take a step forward.

"DISPERSE, HUMANS," he shouts over the malfunctioning robot. "I SHALL SILENCE THIS SHINY AND IRRITATING BEING ONCE AND FOR ALL."

The alien lifts his zap-cannon and aims it right at Björn—our one and only hope of saving the planet.

59.

"WAIT!"

It's what I'm thinking.

But it's not me who shouts it.

It is, improbably, Kermin who, in the nick of time, stops his associate from turning our bot into a pile of shiny dust.

Muckle lowers his zap-cannon and turns to Kermin.

And Kermin points up at the sky.

We all look.

Even Björn—who, thankfully, has all of a sudden shut up.

And what do we see up there in the sky?

A cumulonimbus cloud, sinking toward us.

"Bem," says Dan.

Kermin's gaze snaps back down.

So does Muckle's.

The aliens both glare at Dan.

"Bempulthorpemckrackleflackin?" Kermin   says.

"How do you know Bempulthorpemckrackleflackin?"

Muckle narrows his eyes. Then he aims them back up at the spaceship.

"Oh, that protocol-breaking Plerpian is in a far from insignificant amount of trouble. . . ."

60.

IN THE FORTY OR SO SECONDS IT TAKES FOR

Bem's cloud-covered spaceship to lower down and land on Feldman's Field, I feel just about every emotion imaginable.

Relief.

Fear.

Eagerness.

Fear.

Confusion.

Fear.

Anger.

Fear.

Sadness.

Fear.

Yeah, I guess there's a lot of fear in there.

And a lot of that has to do with not knowing what Muckle means by "trouble," and also just how much a "far from insignificant amount" is to him.

But we're about to find out. . . .

Seconds after Bem's ship settles onto the field, before

the cloud even fully parts to reveal a door, the ramp pokes out and reaches for the ground. And then Bem comes hurrying down it, racing across the field toward all of us.

As soon as he arrives, Muckle jabs an angry finger toward him and says . . .

Well, I actually don't know what he says, because he says it in whatever language is spoken on Plerp-5. To me, it sounds like someone trying to beatbox through a mouthful of cottage cheese. But Muckle's enraged expression, and the finger he keeps wagging in Bem's face, tells me all I need to know about what's going on.

Bem waits for Muckle to finish berating him.

Then he responds—in English, for our benefit.

He says, "But we were wrong. The humans—they're not all stupid and selfish and careless and destructive. Some of them are good. And some of them are *doing* good. I have been watching these particular Earthlings for several weeks now. They are brilliant, highly imaginative beings. They may prove assets to our planet, and to our galaxy as a whole."

With that, he turns to us.

And just loud enough for Dan, Mikaela, John Henry Knox, Jerry, and Edsley to hear, I say:

"Showtime."

61.

I STEP FORWARD.

"This," I tell Kermin and Muckle in my best science fair presentation voice, "is Björn."

The robot's eyes flash in recognition of its name.

"*Greee*-TINGS," he says. "I am—"

Edsley claps the thing on the back before it can say its name—and *keep* on saying it—yet again.

Mikaela steps up next.

"Björn, of course, is a robot," she says. "A robot designed and built by none other than our friend Dan here."

Dan, shy and humble as ever, gives nothing more than a little nod of acknowledgment.

Kermin and Muckle, meanwhile, are now giving the robot a closer look. It's hard to tell, but it seems like they might be appreciating the thing a bit more now that they know it was a human *kid* who created it.

And now here it is . . .

The moment of truth.

John Henry Knox takes the lead.

"As you are no doubt aware," he tells the aliens, "our planet's climate has been changing relatively rapidly and rather dramatically, especially over the course of the past several decades. We"—John Henry Knox sweeps his arm out to indicate me and Dan and Mikaela and Jerry and Edsley—"understand that our species has been contributing to this change, and that the results have been, well, somewhere between calamitous and catastrophic."

Kermin eyes John Henry Knox.

"*You*," he asks, "understand all of that?"

And the way he says it, it's not like he's in disbelief. It's like he's seriously curious. Like, to use his own words, he's once again considering that we're maybe not as stupid and useless as we seem to be—and, what's more, that we might even be somewhat smart and use*ful*. Which might be why he's stopped speaking so slowly and shouting at us in our own language.

Jerry's the one who finally answers the alien's question.

"We do," he says. "And that's why we've programmed Björn here to do what he does."

Now it's Muckle who seems curious.

"Which is . . . ?" he asks.

Dan clears his throat.

"Björn," he commands. "Enter Analysis-Prescription Mode."

"EN-*terrr*-ING AH-nall-is-is *preee*-SCRIP-CHUN *mooode*," says Björn, his eyes blinking with a brand-new rhythm.

"Now, Björn," Dan says. "This old, overgrown field has sat here, neglected and unused, for many years. Is there anything we could do with it? Anything that might, perhaps, benefit both our immediate community and the planet at large?"

The bot's eyes go dark . . .

. . . then light up again like never before. He sweeps his head back and forth, taking in each and every square foot of the field, his bright eyes illuminating the tips of the tall grass and weeds growing here and there. Then Björn crouches down and sinks the sharp tips of his fingers into the ground. Scooping up a clump of the field's dry earth, he opens the door to his stomach and tosses the stuff in. A moment later, a faint whirring sound can be heard from within the bot, followed by a *CLUNK* and a couple of *CLANK*s.

I wince, hoping everything's running smoothly in

there. A single loose gear or busted spring could mean our doom.

Finally, the whirring stops.

And Björn's eyes once again go dark.

I hold my breath as the seconds pass.

And pass.

And keep on passing.

Until, at last, the bot's eyes light up once more.

And he says:

"FER-till-*iiize* the SOY-ull. PLANT veg-et-ab-ulls IN the north-EAST quad-RANT of THE *fiiield*." Björn points to the part of the field he means, just in case anyone doesn't have a handle on their directions. "LET-tuce, egg-PLANT, cu-CUM-*berrr*, and SQUASH have a HIGH prob-ub-il-uh-*teee* of grow-ING *welll*. A RAIN-wat-*errr* CO-lec-tion SYS-tem will AID with PLANTS and re-DUCE water waste. Shall I PRINT con-STRUC-tion *plaaans*?"

"Please do," answers Dan.

Björn turns around, and a small panel in the upside-down trapezoid that is the robot's pelvis slides aside. And even though I know the guy doesn't have any food-cubes inside of him, I can't help but worry, for a fraction of a second, that a turd missile is going to come firing out of the bot's backside like I've seen so many times before. But it's a small square of paper that emerges instead.

Dan grabs the thing before it falls to the ground, then hands it to the aliens.

Kermin accepts it and holds it up so Muckle can see too.

"'Plans for Rainwater Collection System,'" Muckle reads. "Impressive."

Kermin looks up at us and agrees.

"*Highly* impressive," he says.

62.

showing Kermin and Muckle all the other stuff Björn
can do.

Like how you can ask him for directions to anywhere
in the world, and how he'll not only give you them, but
will tell you the most efficient, environmentally friendly
way for you to get where you want to go.

Or how you can give him just about any object—a
paper clip, a rubber band, an old shoelace—and he can
list dozens of ways that you can repurpose the thing.

Finally, we're done.

Well, *almost*.

Last of all, once Dan and Mikaela and Jerry and
John Henry Knox and I are done showing the aliens
everything *we* programmed the bot to do, Edsley steps
up beside Björn.

"*And*," he says, kicking up a foot and perching his
elbow on the robot's shoulder, "he knows more than
260 bean-based recipes."

Both Kermin and Muckle's eyes widen. They look at each other meaningfully, then gaze again at Björn.

That's when Bem speaks up.

"Protocol #10,643," he says.

All of us turn to him, Plerpian demolition crew included.

That's when Bem slips a small, greenish-gray book out of his pocket. And even though I can't decipher the symbols on the cover, I know it must be a copy of the eleventh edition of the *Plerpian Protocols for Planetary Demolition*.

"Protocol #10,643," Bem repeats. Then, tapping the cover of the tiny book, he begins to recite the protocol. "'If, in the course of planetary demolition, new information is uncovered—information that may reveal that the conclusions that said demolition is predicated upon are inaccurate—it is the duty of the demolition crew to—'"

That's as far as Bem gets. Because that's when Kermin and Muckle take over, reciting the rest of the protocol together:

"'—cease demolishing and report information to Planetary Leadership for analysis and consideration.'"

Then, on his own, Kermin says, "It does seem

possible that our Planetary Leadership reached inaccurate conclusions about your species. A possibility, I might add, that I considered once previously, specifically after learning of the majesty of the pupperoni and the human worship of them."

Hearing this, my fear begins to slip away. Because this is *good*. It sounds to me like we actually pulled this off.

But then I turn to Muckle, and see that he doesn't look quite as convinced as his associate. Even worse, he keeps adjusting his grip on his zap-cannon, like he's eager to use it.

The fear all rushes back.

I hold my breath.

"It will take us several days to travel back to Plerp-5 . . . ," Muckle says. "And we are unable to receive broadcasts of *The Bean Show* while traveling at warp speed. . . ."

Kermin frowns.

"This is a fact," he says. "An unfortunate fact."

"There is also much paperwork to be filled out if we claim Protocol #10,643 . . . ," Muckle goes on. "Continuing with our methodical demolition of your planet requires *no* paperwork. . . ."

"Yuck," Kermin says. "Paperwork."

"Recall, Kermin, that particularly pernicious paper cut you obtained last time we were forced to complete paperwork?"

A shiver runs through Kermin's body.

"For several days," he says, "I could not sanitize my hands without suffering substantial irritation."

Oh my God.

Is *this* what it's all going to come down to?

Paperwork?!

I slide my eyes over to Bem, hoping there's some other protocol he can cite, or at least *something* he can say to convince Kermin and Muckle that doing a little paperwork and missing a few episodes of *The Bean Show* might be preferable to methodically obliterating a planet and its nearly eight billion inhabitants. But the young alien looks just as nervous and unsure as I am.

At last, Kermin sighs.

"Mucklemcdunk?" he says. "I believe we should comply with Protocol #10,643." He winces. "And I will agree to complete the associated paperwork, even at the risk of sustaining additional paper cuts."

An endless second drags by . . .

. . . before Muckle loosens his grip on his zap-cannon and says, "Fine."

The breath I'd been holding comes bursting out of me.

"As protocol requires," Muckle says, "we shall return to Plerp-5 and inform our Planetary Leadership of the fully functioning brains of the young human beings we encountered."

"*Thank you*," I say. "Thank you, thank you, thank you."

Muckle acknowledges me with a nod, then turns to Björn. "We will also speak to our Planetary Leadership of your shiny, rather useful creation."

"Or . . . ," says Dan, ". . . you could just take him with you."

"You have additional Björns?" Muckle asks.

"We don't," Dan says. "But we can build another one."

"And if we had more than half a day," says Mikaela, "probably an even *better* one."

Dan nods.

Then adds, "I also think I could use a little break from robots. Like, for a few days, at least."

"If you insist," Muckle says.

He turns to Bem next.

"You have proven yourself very wise, young

Plerpian, and have potentially prevented us from making a rather large—and quite unalterable—mistake. I will make sure your parental units are aware of these facts should they desire to take them into consideration when choosing how long to ground you for your breaking protocol so flagrantly."

Bem *tsks* his tongue.

"Man," he says.

At last, Muckle turns to Kermin, and the aliens share another meaningful look. It's like there's something else, something they've been holding back but have been wanting to bring up all this time.

It's Kermin who finally says, "Might we now discuss what we originally came down here to discuss?"

Oh.

Right.

The fact that I completely lied to them about speaking Dog and there being some big important *dog meeting* this morning.

"Yeah," I say. "About that. I'm sorry I—"

But that's as far as I get.

Because that's when Kermin, now grinning hopefully, says, "Might we attend?"

I stare at him.

"Attend?" I say.

"Yes," he says. "The meeting. The gathering of the pupperonis. That is why we have returned so many hours before *noon*. And that is why we are *here*, at the one and only Feldman's Field."

I go on staring at the alien, not knowing what to do, wondering if it's better or worse that he still hasn't realized that I lied to him, and wondering, too, if he might be so upset to learn it now that he'll go back on all of what he just said and turn the planet into a bunch of dust after all.

Kermin's grin suddenly disappears, faster than if it got zapped by his zap-cannon.

"Oh dear," he says. "Have we missed it? Has the canine conference already occurred?"

"Um," I say. "Uhh. Well. You see. I—I, ah—"

I cock my head to the side.

Did I really hear what I think I just heard, or was that wishful thinking?

But there it is again.

Faint.

But growing louder.

And louder.

And louder still.

RARF!

Rarf-rarf-rarf!

Ruff-ruff-ruff-ruff RARF!

Kermin gasps.

His grin grows even bigger.

"Is it—" he asks. "Is that—"

But he's too excited to even get the rest of the words out.

And there's no need for him to, anyway.

Seconds later, his question is answered.

RARF!

RARF-RUFF-RARF!

RUFF-RUFF-RUFF-RUFF RARF-RARF-RARF!

A pack of dogs comes tearing around the corner and charging out onto the field.

And who's in front, leading them all? Kitty.

How?

I don't have a clue.

But I'm too grateful to see him to even care.

The dogs chase one another around in great big

looping circles all across the field, barking at and with and over one another. They're having the time of their lives.

So is Kermin.

He looks as delighted as a creature—human, Plerpian, or *whatever*—can be.

Eventually, he manages to tear his eyes off the dogs long enough to look at me again.

"What are they saying?" he asks me, his voice a whisper, as if he might somehow interrupt the very important dog business occurring on the other side of the field.

I tip my ear toward the dogs, like I'm concentrating hard on their *RARF*s.

Then I tell Kermin, "They're asking you to join them."

The alien's mouth falls open. But no words come out. He's too overwhelmed to speak.

Finally, he lifts a finger, aims it at his chest, raises his eyebrows inquiringly.

I pretend to listen to the dogs again. "Yep," I tell the alien. "You."

And that's all the alien needs. He shoves his zap-cannon into Muckle's hand and hurries out to meet the dogs, his tie flying over his shoulder like a bright, striped flag. He runs and jumps and laughs and screams, and even lets out a few *RARF*s of his own.

We all watch him, enjoying the alien's joy from afar.

Then Muckle says, "Oh, all right."

He tucks his and Kermin's zap-cannons into the band of his underpants, then hurries out to join his associate and the dogs.

Edsley's the next to go.

Followed by Jerry.

And Bem.

Even Björn.

Then John Henry Knox.

Finally, it's just me, Dan, and Mikaela standing there, watching the joyous commotion taking place on the other end of the field.

"Shall we?" asks Dan.

And Mikaela and I—we say it at the same exact time:

"RARF!"

With that, we run, laughing and shouting and barking our lungs out for the whole universe to hear.

Epilogue

THAT'S IT.

That's really all there is to tell.

Eventually, the dogs got tired and ran back to their respective homes.

Kermin and Muckle boarded their ship, Björn in tow.

And Bem left too, after we thanked him, like, ten thousand times for helping to save our butts—not to mention the butts of the billions of other people on our planet.

He didn't say bye to us, which was interesting.

Instead he said, "I'll be seeing you."

But that was six weeks ago. We watched his cloud-covered spaceship rise up into the sky and disappear, and we haven't seen or heard from him since.

I can only assume that our plan worked. That Kermin and Muckle and Bem—and, of course, Björn—did and said enough to convince the leaders of Plerp-5 to spare our planet, to find somewhere else for their ginormongous bean billboard to go.

That's the thing, though—we can only assume.

Which is why we've been on our very best behavior ever since. Why we've been doing everything we can to take care of our precious, precious planet, and to convince others to do the same. Why we've been trying, basically, to be the greatest galactic neighbors that ever did exist.

It's why we're now spending our Saturday afternoon at the one and only Feldman's Field, our hands and knees covered in dirt, our backs aching, our muscles sore. Because just a few days after Björn soared up into the sky with Kermin and Muckle and Bem, we took the bot's advice, and got to work turning that neglected expanse of patchy grass into a garden. We didn't have Björn to help, of course, but we managed pretty well on our own.

We sampled the dirt and used a few of Mikaela's gadgets to analyze the stuff and figure out just what sort of nutrients it needed before it could serve as half-decent soil. We gathered up a bunch of wood and built beds in the spots that got just the right amount of sunshine and shade. We even spent a couple days collecting fertilizer, hanging out at the dog park and—well, you probably don't want to hear any more about that. Let's just say we've got ourselves a thriving compost pile.

Kitty, perhaps unsurprisingly, likes to take naps right beside the thing.

We don't have much to show for all our hard work— at least not *yet*. There are just a handful of small, bright green leaves poking up out of the dark brown earth. But that still feels like an accomplishment, and we're all pretty darn proud of it.

"Cloud!"

It's Edsley, shouting out from the other side of the field, where he and some of the other EngiNerds are doing maintenance on our rainwater collection system.

And all of us—each and every one of the EngiNerds, and even Kitty—look up at the enormous, curiously shaped cumulonimbus cloud cruising across the sky. It doesn't slow down. It doesn't sink. It just continues on its way.

We all watch it, silently wondering upward, for a full minute. Or maybe for even longer. It's hard to tell. Time stretches and bends in weird ways when you get to wondering like that.

But then someone shouts, "Anyone got a Phillips-head screwdriver?" and the spell is broken.

Someone else calls out, "Right here! I'll bring it over!"

We lower our heads and get back to work.

Acknowledgments

THANK YOU TO MY FAMILY AND FRIENDS FOR all the love, support, and encouragement—especially Danni and Isla, without whose love, support, and encouragement I wouldn't accomplish a single thing.

Thank you to Myrsini Stephanides, who always has my back and never bats an eye at my often off-the-wall ideas.

Thank you to Karen Nagel, who helps me turn my ideas into books—books that wouldn't be even half as good without her.

Thank you to Karin Paprocki and Serge Seidlitz, the masterminds behind all the staggeringly excellent EngiNerds art.

Thank you to everyone else at Simon & Schuster/ Aladdin who had a hand in making this book what it is, and thank you to everyone there who has promoted and/or celebrated the EngiNerds series.

Thank you to Mike Lowery's fantastic *Random Illustrated Facts*, from which I took the random facts that John Henry Knox shares with Ken and Mikaela in Chapter 13.

Thank you to every educator, librarian, bookseller, parent, and other person who has helped get my books into the hands of young readers.

And thank you to my readers, every single kid who has picked up *EngiNerds*, *Revenge of the EngiNerds*, or *The EngiNerds Strike Back*, who has spent some time with my words, exploring this little world I've created. I hope these books have given you at least a fraction of the joy, hope, and inspiration that you have given me.

About the Author

JARRETT LERNER LIKES BEANS (GREAT
Northern and garbanzo are two of his favorite varieties) but does NOT like planetary destruction (no matter what the variety). He lives with his family in Medford, Massachusetts. You can visit him online at jarrettlerner.com and on Twitter and Instagram @Jarrett_Lerner.